Jake Rains

1898 Cuba! When his best friend and fellow Rough Rider lies fatally wounded, Jake Rains swears to care for his widow. The trouble is Kitty Cartright already has a protector, Chris Leeward, owner of the L double E ranch.

Things don't look good when Jake arrives in Oakum. There is trouble at the Cartright place, but Jake and his new friend, Sam, are determined to put things right. Not only are they faced with Leeward's cruel riders, a band of zealous mountain men lusting for vengeance, but also the advent of the most modern of inventions. The challenge calls for old-fashioned courage on the streets of Oakum where Jake Rains must fight for his life.

Jake Rains

Tony Masero

A Black Horse Western

ROBERT HALE · LONDON

ISBN 978-0-7090-9301-5

Robert Hale Limited
Clerkenwell House
Clerkenwell Green
London EC1R 0HT

www.halebooks.com

*The first one for Luke, Sebastian and Joshua
may there be many more*

Typeset by
Derek Doyle & Associates, Shaw Heath
Printed and bound in Great Britain by
CPI Antony Rowe, Chippenham and Eastbourne

PROLOGUE

Jake Rains crouched by the side of his best friend as he lay dying.

Around them bullets whined down from the top of Kettle Hill where the Spanish held the high ground. Shells exploded overhead cascading a rain of hot fragments through the hanging battle smoke. A mist so dense it stung the eyes and kept the rest of the Rough Riders from clear view along the shallow riverbed where they sheltered. They were pinned down here, waiting for the order to attack and slowly being decimated by the tardiness of command.

Jake's throat was dry as he looked over at Calum with a worried frown. The wounded soldier lay with a spreading flow of blood from the wound in his chest where a Mauser 7mm rifle bullet had pierced him clear through the breast. Blood bubbled from Calum's lips and Jake knew the young man was breathing his last as the lungs slowly flooded.

Turning away, Jake angrily fired a few vain shots from his carbine towards the distant smoke-cloaked buildings atop the hill.

'Jake! Jake!' The husked whisper called his attention back to his companion.

'Yes, old pal. What is it?'

'You got any water left?'

Jake shook his head in frustration. 'Not a drop. I'm sorry.'

'No matter.'

Calum Cartright was in his twenty-fourth year and a calm young fellow, given his circumstances. They had been friends since answering the call for volunteers in the jingoistic wave that had swept the Southern states in answer to President McKinley's stirring call for independence from Spain on the island of Cuba. The two young men had enlisted in the 1st US Volunteer Cavalry in that year of 1898 and it was Jake who had come to owe Calum his life on more than one occasion amidst the tangled vines of the sniper-ridden jungle, once they were dismounted and had been relegated to an infantryman's role.

'There's something you must do for me,' Calum panted painfully.

'What's that, Cal?'

'When I'm gone . . .' weakly he brushed aside Jake's reassurance even before it was made. 'My wife. She'll need help. I worry for her on the place all alone. Will you see to her wellbeing?'

Jake strained to hear his friend's soft words over the sounds of rifle- and shell-fire. 'Of course. But you'll be there yourself, I'll get you back; don't worry on that score.'

Calum shook his head and offered a thin cynical smile. 'I think not. My day is done. But you will see to Kitty's welfare, won't you? Promise me that.'

'On my life,' Jake promised grimly, 'if I live that long.'

'Swear it,' Calum hissed forcefully, clutching Jake's shirt-sleeve. 'On your honour, for now she will have no other to help her in this world.'

'I do, Calum. I do.'

'It's a pretty place,' Calum said dreamily. 'You'll like. . . .' His voice faded away to stillness.

Jake watched his friend's eyes finally glaze over and stare unseeing into the destroyed sky above them. Jake clenched his jaw in bitterness and looked towards the foe. A burning anger beat in his breast now, that and a hard desire for vengeance.

'Come on, lads!' It was the lieutenant-colonel, old Teddy,

rearing fearlessly above them on his white horse, hat in hand and waving them boldly on. His round-lensed spectacles flashed in the sunlight and the broad spread of his square-cut, gate-mouthed teeth were bared as he screamed the command: 'Attack!'

The cry was carried by sergeants along the spread line and they rose up in a wave of blue flannel shirts, the flags spinning out and whipping above them in the sultry air. With a roar the men of the Rough Riders climbed from the river bank with a willing relief at being finally released. There was not a man amongst them who did not burn with fervour and the desire to fight. They came from all walks of life: dentists, teachers, cowhands and stockyarders, and they ran forward side by side, all of them alive with the wildness of battle. Climbing the rough pockmarked hillside, littered with the empty sugar refinement cauldrons that gave it its name, they followed after the determined stocky figure of Teddy Roosevelt as he hallooed them on.

Many had come at first just for the fun of it, for the adventure and thrill of the conflict, and they meant to have their way. Now though that was forgotten as a murderous fire rained down on them; but still they maintained their steady upward climb of the steep hill, dropping and pausing only momentarily to fire their rifles, then moving onward again. Jake clenched his jaw and his eyes still burned with the desire for bloody vengeance. The uneven ground blossomed into explosions of dust, and passing bullets cracked around him as his young limbs skipped from cover to cover. The sun burned hot above and the baked soil crumbled in places under his boots. Sweat streamed down Jake's unshaven cheeks but he barely noticed, his intention set only on reaching that summit and offering some bloody payback for his lost friend to the Spanish defenders.

They broke through the outer defensive fencing and Jake climbed over the fallen body of one of his companions which lay like a bridge over the wire, to run on and take part in the hand-to-hand fighting he could see taking place behind the sandbag

emplacements that encircled the buildings. It was a vicious strug-
gle, fast and furious, with little time to consider anything other
than the opponent who reared up in front. Men fell around
Jake, beaten by rifle butt, bayonet or bullet. The Americans continued to pour over the hilltop, crashing open the doors to the
outhouses and shooting down the inhabitants where they found
them.

Once overrun, many of the blueshirts knelt at the crest and
potted at the retreating Spaniards, who ran wildly down the far
side of the hill trying to make for the sister height of San Juan.
It was a rabbit hunt for the Americans, country boys who took a
delight in the number they could fell and counted scored
accordingly.

Jake leant back tiredly against an adobe wall with the rest of
the advance soldiers, all of them exhausted. He looked down to
see a bloody bayonet in his hand, his wrist and arm were soaked
to the elbow. He had no recollection of how the weapon had got
there. His hat was gone and his shirt torn. Numbly he rubbed at
the encrustations of dust and spattered blood that stained his
cheek. At his feet lay a fallen Spanish artilleryman, the white
tunic stained with black gunpowder burns from the guns they
could not depress far enough to fire on the advancing troops
climbing the final yards of the steep hill. The body had a canteen
attached to its waist belt and Jake snatched the container
thirstily, drinking the contents in continuous gulps until it was
dry.

It was not water, he realized then, but wine. The sour taste did
nothing to alleviate his thirst but only echoed his disdain for the
images of death that surrounded him. It was a shock for him to
find his earlier killing lust dissipate so quickly. To fall into a hol-
lowness that did no justice to Calum or to the obscure cause they
followed here in Cuba.

Jake let the bloodstained bayonet slip from his fingers and fall
to the ground.

'Bully, boys, bully!' It was Teddy Roosevelt standing before him with a smoking pistol in his hand, his cheeks flaming red and his eyes dancing with a fire that matched the broad grin on his face. 'Never seen such bold brass, men. And you, sir,' he waved his pistol in Jake's direction, 'a veritable hero, sir. As a Greek champion of old you cut them down before you like a scythe in the cornfield. I'll have your name, sir?'

Jake faltered, suddenly brought back from his gloomy thoughts. 'Why, it's Trooper Jake Rains, Colonel.'

'Volunteer Rains, mark this day. Remember it well. For today you proved your mettle here, so hold your head high, young fellow. You're one of the warrior elect, indeed you are. Now then,' he paused, already demonstrating a natural politician's ability for timing. Then, softly. 'Will you follow me on?'

Jake managed a smile at the man's irresistible drive. 'I will, sir.'

Teddy Roosevelt roared a loud contented laugh. 'Then come along. There is another hill we must take. There,' he waved his pistol. 'The San Juan Heights awaits us. Let's show we can do it again and drive these damned Spaniards clear into hell or the sea. What say you?'

The gathered Rough Riders, their exhaustion forgotten, cheered with an eagerness that only a willing and bold commander can raise and together they followed as their leader ran before them. Once again Jake felt a surge run through his breast at being one with such a brave band and, clutching his carbine in both hands, he set off over the breast of the hill and into the valley below. He realized then there was no distant cause here for consideration, it was far closer to home. There was only companionship. A band of brothers, a sense that reinforced the promised bond with his lost companion lying in the ditch below them.

CHAPTER ONE

Jake Rains pulled his pony to a standstill on the tree lined hilltop and looked down at the valley township of Oakum. A goodly sized town, grown from an old buffalo hunter's trading post alongside the broad flat-banked river that ran the length of the valley. Well ordered, with a clean wide main street, Jake noticed. Split timber- and mud-brick-built houses populated the suburbs and petered out towards scattered smallholding plots beyond the town boundaries. Wooded countryside formed a natural barrier on each sloping side of the wide valley and gave Oakum a comfortable and welcoming feel. Jake liked the look of the place.

He geed the pony on and began his descent. Jake was already fond of this darkly copper-coloured mare who showed a natural and intelligent talent in response to his direction. There was a wild streak there though, and when the beast took it in mind it could be mule-stubborn if the task did not appeal. This was probably why he had managed to hold onto the creature on his release from the army back in August, when the Rough Riders were disbanded. He had taken to calling the mare Penny in light of its colouring. Officially, all equipment was supposed to be returned to the government up there in Long Island but like so many others Jake still hung on to some of his gear. He kept a new blue shirt and tan pants, a broom-handled Mauser pistol he had taken from a dead German adviser and the Krag-Jorgensen-issue carbine holstered in his saddle sheath. Jake reckoned he had earned it.

The narrow trail he was on crossed the main road into the town, and it was at this junction that he met a loaded oxen-pulled freight wagon, which was travelling in. The old driver eyed him suspiciously as Jake pulled alongside.

'Help you?' asked the grizzled bullwhacker around a jawful of chewing tobacco.

'Sure. Looking for the Cartright place. You know it?'

The old man spat a stream to one side. 'I know it. What you want there? Ain't nothing there.'

Jake shrugged noncommittally. 'Where's it at?'

'Ride on through town. Get on about ten mile due west. You'll see her.'

'Obliged.'

As Jake took his leave and rode on in ahead of the wagon he noticed the town's amenities were plentiful. There was a 'Six Bit House', a stage stopover with floor space advertised at fifty cents a head with supper, bed and breakfast at twenty-five cents. A butcher shop offered patrons beef and bear steak, buffalo hump and prairie chicken. A drug and cigar store had a soda fountain and patent medicines on offer. The Leeward Trust Bank and Livery Stable dispensed paper money as well as hay and grain, a boot-and-shoe supplier promised clothing for all and there was even a Chinaman's small store stood set off to one side on its lonesome. In all the town seemed to offer anything a body could desire.

Jake stopped at the Leeward General Store and tied up to the long hitching rail, letting the mare drink its fill from the deep water-filled zinc trough laid out in front. He climbed up plank steps to the freshly swept wooden boardwalk and entered the shop. It was an open, fair-sized white-painted interior, high ceilinged and bulging with produce. Jake drew in the pleasant smell of calico and candy that permeated the well-stocked

11

shelves. Customers bustled about him, gloved farmhands gingerly handling rolls of barbed wire and housewives debated the value of various newly arrived wallpaper and patterned bolts of cloth. Jake took his time studying the occupants and getting a feel for the nature of the place.

'Help you, stranger?' The clerk finally got around to him. A slender, nervy young man with wispy fair hair centre-parted under the peak of a green celluloid eyeshade.

'I'd like some supplies.'

'Surely. Name your pleasure.'

'Guess I'll take me a sack of beans, flour, side of bacon. Loaf of that home-baked bread. Some of them tins of fruit and canned fish you got there. Rolling tobacco too. You sell spirits here?'

'No, sir. That'll be over at the drinking house. Across the street.'

'Fair enough. Set me up, will you, and I'll be back directly.'

'Be ready when you get here. Is that all?'

'For now.'

The bar of the Barrel of Beer was like the rest of the town, wide and roomy. A long, dark, wooded bartop stretched the length of the low ceilinged room, and gilt-framed artistic renditions of the old droving days hung from the panelled walls behind. It was gloomy inside, even though it was mid-afternoon, the lamps not being lit yet awhile. To the rear of the room was an area obviously set aside for gaming: a table was in play with a few diehard gamblers throwing well worn paste cards over green baize. The rest of the place was empty except for a couple of lone farming customers sipping silently on mugs of beer and taking their time over seed catalogues and newsheets.

'What'll it be?' asked the bartender, a burly, apron-clad fellow with macassar-oiled hair and a hefty moustache, waxed and curled at the tips.

'Some of that rye whiskey you've got there.'

'Shot, or you want the bottle?'

'Set me up two short ones, will you? That'll do it for now. I'll take a bottle with me though.'

Deftly the barman clinked up two shot-glasses and poured the drink into one and then the other without pausing.

'Nice town you got here,' observed Jake.

'We like it. You passing through?'

'Uhuh.'

'There's plenty to do, if you're looking for something. Place is growing. Mr Leeward, our main benefactor is always on the lookout for hands who ain't workshy.'

'Mr Leeward?'

The barman wiped his hands over his white apron as if straightening creases. 'Sure, Chris Leeward. Cattle rancher. Runs the L-Double-E spread outside of town. Fine gentleman. Done a lot for this place. Nice fellow too. Keeps his men happy; you should try him if you've a mind. He has an office open most days here on Main Street.'

Jake shook his head. 'I seen his name up there on the billboards. But no thanks, I'm taken care of.'

The bartender raised a full bottle from behind the counter and placed it cautiously in front of Jake. 'You do have the where-withal for this, don't you, cowboy?'

Jake looked up at him a long moment. 'Sure do, partner. Enough severance pay for this and a few more if I was so inclined.' He spread coin on the bartop as proof.

'Right you are,' said the barman, sweeping up the money. 'No offence. Severance pay, you say, Army man?'

'Some. Down there in Cuba a while.'

The bartender's eyes widened in appreciation. 'Rough Rider, huh? You were with old Teddy, were you?'

'Sure was. He spoke right to me one day. Right there on top of the Kettle Hill.'

'Hell, you don't say. Here fellow, have one on the house. You boys did a fine job down there.'

'No thank you, sir. Two's my limit. I have things to do and I need to keep my head clear.'

'Well, well.' The barman grinned broadly. 'A Rough Rider right here in this saloon, don't that beat all.'

Jake smiled vaguely in response and threw back his first shot. The whiskey warmed his insides and he appreciated the glow. It had been a long time.

'So, what's he like, old Teddy?' the barman asked, leaning on folded arms over the bartop with an inquisitive gleam in his eye.

Jake toyed with the rim of his second glass. 'He's a gamecock, all right. Bold as they get.'

'And that run up the hill. I read in the paper. Man, it sounded right glorious.'

Jake's eyes blanked as he remembered Calum's sad end. He raised his glass and drained it. 'Not so you'd notice,' he said coldly. 'Just lead and death really, nothing glorious at all.'

'But I seen the illustrated pictures, flags waving and our brave boys charging. Did me proud to say I was American.'

'But then,' Jake lowered his glass, taking his bottle by the neck, 'you wasn't there, was you?'

Jake was making his way across the broad main street heading back to the store when a voice called out to him from behind. 'Hey there! Young fellow. Hold up, will you?'

Jake turned to see a pinch-faced, stringy-looking fellow in a long drape coat with a heavy tin star dragging down the lapel.

'Help you, Sheriff?'

The scrawny fellow came up close to Jake and spoke quietly. 'We don't like this kind of thing here in Oakum,' he said.

'What kind of thing would that be, sir?'

The sheriff shook his head. He wore a broad-brimmed black Stetson with the crown punched out and had more the appearance of a sad looking preacher than a law officer. 'We're a decent town. Don't hold with cowhands holding liquor bottles out here in Main Street. You want to drink you do it in the saloon, not here with folks about, you hear?'

'I just did that,' said Jake amiably. 'I'm making my way over to the store there to pick up the rest of my purchases. This here bottle ain't for drinking right now.'

The sheriff gave Jake a searching slow up and down look. 'Where you headed, boy?'

'Away from here.'

'Well, that's fine. You do that. No place for itinerants here.'

Jake frowned wryly. 'You're a right welcoming gent, ain't you?'

The sheriff looked past Jake then at the empty street around him. He pulled back the front of his coat to expose the holstered pistol high on his waist. 'The name's Younghusband Deeling; maybe you heard of me?'

Jake shrugged. 'Can't say that I have.'

Sheriff Deeling looked a little miffed at that. He frowned and urged Jake on with a nod of his head, 'You just head along now, son.'

'I aim to,' said Jake turning to go.

'And keep that bottle out of sight,' said Sheriff Deeling to his back.

Shaking his head, Jake obediently tucked the whiskey under his arm and went on over to the store.

The countryside rolled away pleasantly from Jake as he rode south out of town. Green and lush, it was prime cattle country and herds of crossbred Herefords and Longhorns roamed freely, fattening themselves on the long summer grass. In the distance the soft blue of mountain ranges stood proud on the skyline, their definition lost in a late afternoon mellow haze. Pockets of blue spruce and juniper peppered the roadside and the humming sound of busy insects filled the air. It all gave Jake a calming sense of contentment. Even the run-in with the cantankerous lawman was forgotten as he allowed Penny to walk along at her own easy own pace.

He noticed that many of the roaming cattle had the LEE brand on their hides and was not surprised when a bunch of cowhands rode into view hustling the beef back onto their own range. Hooking a leg over the saddle horn, Jake rolled a spill of tobacco and settled to watch the cowhands as they drove the loose steers across the roadway before him. A trio of men separated from the herd and rode towards him, pulling up and blocking the way ahead.

'You got business here, stranger?' one of them asked abruptly. He was a dark-faced, unshaven individual with a long scarf bandanna slung over his shoulder and a battered campaign hat on his head, the brim rolled up in front.

Jake zipped a match across his boot sole and lit up. 'Not with you,' he answered calmly, blowing smoke skywards.

'This here is L-Double-E land you're on,' the fellow offered gruffly.

'Looks like a public highway to me.'

'Then where you headed on it?'

Slowly, Jake unhitched his leg and found the stirrup with his boot toe. ' 'Pears to me, everybody wants to know my business in this neighbourhood. I don't ask you yourn, why in hell should I tell you mine.'

One of the others moved his pony forward, brushing aside his rude companion. 'Pay no heed to old Cole here, mister. He gets a burr in his blanket some days. It's just we've had some trouble with cow-thieving lately, is all. Name's Buck Holdall.' He held out his hand as he came alongside Jake. 'Pleased to meet you.'

Jake took the offered hand. 'Jake Rains. Likewise, I'm sure.'

Buck Holdall was a good-looking young man with an open face and long, dark sideburns lying under the leather strap that kept his flat-topped-crown hat in place. 'This handsome buckaroo alongside me here is Lorn Chaser.' Buck introduced a silent, unpleasant-looking fellow with a hooded, pockmarked face, hook nose and a cast in one eye. 'And Cole Reichter you already met.'

Reichter sneered and pushed up his hat brim, exposing coldly expressionless pale eyes. 'So,' he pressed. 'Now we got the

16

niceties out the way I still want to know where you headed.'

'I'm making for the Cartright place, if it's any business of yours.'

'Why,' said Buck lightly, ignoring his pushy companion, 'You're almost there. It's just down the road apiece. Couple of hills yonder and you're there. You know the widow Cartright?'

'Nope. Knew her husband though.'

'Uhuh, Army then. I heard he passed down in Cuba with the Riders.'

'That's the truth of it.'

'You'll be offering your condolences then?'

Jake could see that, despite his friendly front, Buck was in fact a far subtler questioner than his rough partner Cole Reichter, yet behind the veil of polite conversation his intentions were exactly the same.

'Something like that,' Jake answered.

'Don't think the widow's to home, Jake. Her and Mr Leeward are pretty tight these days. Could be she'll be visiting with him right now.'

Cole Reichter chuckled slyly at that. Buck turned swiftly and gave him a withering glance that froze the smile on the cowhand's face.

'I'll just go take a looksee,' said Jake, wondering what the story was here.

'Sure enough. You go on right ahead. Come on, Cole. Let the man through, get your sorry ass out the way. We got beeves to go get.'

Reluctantly Reichter moved his pony aside and Jake pressed on. 'You take care now, won't you?' Reichter sneered softly as Jake passed by him.

'Don't worry on that score, mister,' Jake replied coldly, not liking the fellow at all.

'See you around,' Buck called, then with a whoop he laid spur to his pony and galloped off, leading the other two in the direction of the scattered cattle.

*

Jake crested the last hill and saw the Cartright ranch spread out on lower ground below him. It gave him a shock of consternation to see the condition of the place. Run-down and untended, the corral fences were broken and fallen in places. The main house was overgrown with creepers right to the rooftop and the paintwork was peeling and sad looking. A decaying wooden picket fence swayed and sagged before what once had been a kitchen garden, now overgrown with a mass of weeds and wild goldenrod standing waist high. A barn stood to one side of the main corral and planks were missing from the walls, leaving gaps where the afternoon sun slanted through and showed forgotten and cobweb coated tackle hanging tangled inside. Above the open barn doors a weathered but once-smooth shingle swung by a single rusty nail. The words THE CARTRIGHT HOLDING had been burnt into the surface with a hot iron. Now the wood was cracked and grey, its varnished surface long since worn away.

It was a sorry picture of neglect and it pained Jake to see it so, as he remembered Calum's glowing descriptions. Jake rode up to the house and dismounted out front, allowing Penny's reins to hang loose, knowing she would not wander as he explored the dilapidated building. The front door was unlocked and creaked open to his touch. He entered a large, bare living room where the sun broke through the dirty windows and cast mote-filled golden beams over the dust-laden floorboards and soot-strewn stone fireplace. There were other rooms leading off the main one: a kitchen area and two other rooms. One of these was obviously a bedroom, as the frame of a large, heavy, home-made pine bedstead stood leaning against the wall.

'Damn,' muttered Jake to himself. 'What the hell happened here?' He stood, pondering for a moment. Then, making up his mind, he decisively went back outside and unsaddled Penny. He led the mare to the broken corral, put her inside, fed her and saw she had enough pump water available from a trough. He made good the fallen posts of unstripped pinewood as best he could to keep the mare from wandering. Then, with his saddle, blanket, rifle and supplies, he returned to the house, cleared a space and made ready to bunk down for the coming night. There was plenty of loose timber lying around, so he soon had a fire going in the stone fireplace. That gave some element of cheer to the deserted place.

Later, as he watched the firelight flicker on the empty walls he decided on his course of action. He had promised to care for Cal's widow, to see she was set all right, and he intended to keep his word. No doubt he would run into the woman sooner or later but until that day there was plenty to occupy him here, putting the place in order. At first light he would begin the repairs.

CHAPTER TWO

The morning dawned with a pearly sky and a low mist that softened the tree line and hid the horizon from view. There was a whinny of greeting from Penny as Jake doused himself in the trough and allowed the cold water to bring him to life. The air was brisk with a slight chill that refreshed Jake and he drew deeply of the cool pine scent as he looked over the house and decided where to start. The roof was the obvious place, loose and missing tiles were letting in rainwater. A stack of bark tiles lay against a side wall ready for such an eventuality and although the top layers had rotted through, lower in the stack Jake found whole ones substantial enough for the task. Rolling up his sleeves, Jake set to.

He was up a ladder hard at work replacing the missing roof tiles when the stranger came by. A tall man, lean-faced with a full drooping moustache, he sat stooped in the saddle, his clothes white with the dust of travel and his gear showing signs of rough usage.

'Say there!' the man called, startling Jake who had not heard the visitor's approach over the noise of his hammering.

Jake turned and eyed the man cautiously. 'What can I do for you?' he asked.

'Mind if I water my horse?'

'Sure. Help yourself. Water over by the corral.'

'Obliged.'

The stranger turned his pony away towards the corral and plodded tiredly over. He had an air about him, Jake decided. Tired he was, that was for sure, but there was something firm and resolute about the man's posture that shone through his exhaustion. Jake was about to return to his work when he saw the man dismount and stagger as he did so, almost losing his balance and falling to the ground.

Resolutely, the fellow recovered himself, loosened his horse's cinch and allowed it to drink. The beast looked as done in as its owner.

' 'Bout to make some breakfast,' Jake called as he descended the ladder. 'Care to join me?'

'Kind of you,' husked the man. 'But we'll be getting along. Don't want to be no trouble.'

'No trouble, it's only beans, bacon and biscuits. You're welcome to it.'

The fellow rubbed his jaw and looked at Jake from under the brim of his hat as if assessing the invite. Then he snorted a tired laugh. 'Won't say I can't use it. Thanks.'

'That pony of yours is plumb tuckered out. Let him loose in the corral alongside my mare. There's feed in the barn. Come on in when you're done.'

The man nodded and Jake went on into the house, pausing at the doorway. 'Name's Jake Rains, by the way.'

'Sam Parks,' the stranger replied. 'Thanks again, Mr Rains.'

While he prepared the food Jake watched the man through the window as he dusted himself off and sluiced his face in the water trough. He tended the pony tenderly and led it into the corral, patting the animal's neck and whispering to it gently as he went.

Jake had found an old table and chairs stored in the back of the barn and brought them into the house. He laid out tin plates and had coffee brewing by the time the man appeared at the door.

'Mind if I come in?'

'Sit yourself,' Jake said. 'Be ready right off.'

Sam Parks took off his hat, unhitched the pistol belt he wore and hung them over the back of a chair. He watched Jake as he fried up thick slices of bacon.

'Sure smells good,' he observed.

21

'Help yourself to coffee. You sure look tired, Mr Parks. Reckon you've done some hard travelling.'

'That's a fact, sir. Been looking for work awhile. Know of anything around here?'

Jake hustled over to the table and sliced healthy portions of beans and bacon onto Parks' plate. 'Depends on your inclinations. There's store work in the town, I guess. Big spread near by too, if you fancy cowboying.'

Sam Parks took a sip from his steaming coffee mug. 'That so? Maybe I should go take a looksee for myself.'

'Well, tuck in.'

'Real good of you, Mr Rains.'

'Call me Jake.' He reached across the table and they shook. It was a firm resolute hand Jake received, calloused and rock steady.

They sat and began to eat. Jake could not help but observe that Sam wolfed his food down as if he were afraid it would run off the plate.

'I apologize, Jake,' Sam said, noticing the glance. 'Got to admit I'm a little low on funds right now. Ain't eaten well in three days.'

'Go to it, mister. Don't mind me, you just get your fill. I've been there and know how it is.'

Jake placed the man in his fifties although it was hard to tell accurately as his weathered features and lean frame hindered a true determination of his age. Later, when they were finished and were enjoying a smoke over their coffee, Sam leaned back and looked around as if it were the first time he had noticed his surroundings.

'Sure feels better,' he said, patting his flat stomach. 'This here is a nice spread you've got yourself, Jake. Looks like you're starting to bring her up to scratch right now.'

'Oh, it ain't mine. Belongs to the wife of a buddy of mine. I'm just fixing things.'

'That so? Well if you need a hand I'm available.'

Jake chuckled. 'I could certainly do with it but I'm as broke as you, partner. Couldn't pay you a single cent I'm afraid.'

Sam rubbed his jaw and brushed the ends of his moustache, which was a habit he seemed to have when he was thinking.

'Jake,' he said at last, 'you seem an upright fellow, so I'll be straight with you. I need a place real bad right now. Found and keep would be fine with me. I'm a hard worker and I'll do right by you.'

Jake remained silent, mulling the notion over. He felt a natural liking for the man and could see he was capable. He also liked the way he had observed him treating his pony outside, it exampled a tendency for care and respect.

'Well, maybe, Sam. You appreciate there ain't much here in the way of home comforts just yet.'

'Don't matter none. One thing though . . .' he paused a moment. 'You have to know this, wouldn't be right if I didn't tell you. There's people on my trail.'

'Looked like you were running hard.'

'I done no legal wrong but they don't see it that way.'

'Mind telling me?'

'It's a family thing,' Sam said vaguely. 'There's been blood and I'm running 'cause I don't want to be the reason for more.'

'Well, Sam, that's your affair and I won't pry. But, what the hell, let's give it a go.'

A thin smile cracked Sam's steady face. 'You got a deal.' He reached across the table and they shook on it.

'You know Jake,' said Sam later as he hauled away tendrils of the rampant vine growing up the house walls. 'I seen wild mustang on my way up here. Might be a thing worth following up. Heard the army is looking for regular mounts.'

'Mm,' said Jake from the rooftop. 'That's not a bad idea. Could certainly do with the income. How far off d'you see them?'

'Away yonder,' Sam pointed in the direction of the mountains. 'In the foothills. About two days' easy ride.'

Jake crouched on the sloping roof and looked off at the vein of pale blue that marked the range.

'Close enough. We'll do it when we fixed up a good-sized corral. You any good at breaking?'

'Been a while. I'll give it a try, though maybe my old bones ain't up to it just yet awhile.'

'How many years you carrying, then?'

'Close as I can figure somewhere between fifty and sixty; can't say I'm right sure though.'

'That'd put you around twenty when the War Between the States started.'

'Yep, I was there, fighting for the Union. Went right through with nary a scratch to speak of. Did some Indian fighting too, right after.'

They worked on through the day, stopping only for a brief bite at lunchtime. By evening the roof was finished and a high pile of weeds was ready for burning when they had dried out.

'Good day's work,' observed Jake as they stood on the veranda and shared a slug from the whiskey bottle he had bought earlier in town. 'We're going to need more supplies now there's the two of us. I'll get into town tomorrow and pick some up. Can you stay here and start on the corral?'

'Sure, I'll do it. Good thing about this place is there's no shortage of jack pine around.'

The bottle passed again. 'So is your friend's wife footing the bill for all this?' Sam asked.

'No, it's not that way,' Jake answered, looking off to the sunset. 'Cal took a bullet in Cuba and passed. It was his dying wish I care for the place and his widow. Cal was a good companion and true friend so I swore I would do it. Haven't met his widow yet. Don't rightly know where she is; I thought she'd be here when I rode in couple of days back.'

Sam looked at him over the bottle neck with a appraising glance. 'You're a man of your word then, Jake?'

Jake shrugged. 'What else is there? Man don't mean nothing unless he keeps to his say-so.'

Sam nodded approvingly. 'You're right there, partner.

Though these days there's not many others that feel the same, I reckon.'

'Don't matter to me, Sam. That's my way and that's all there is to it.'

CHAPTER THREE

Chris Leeward looked out through his office window and watched Kitty Cartright cross Main Street and make her way towards him. Leeward considered her to be a fine looking woman, with her ringleted golden hair, free of any bonnet and coiling luxuriously around her handsome features in the slight breeze. He had been fascinated with her since the first time he had seen her three years before when he had arrived in Oakum. The departure and subsequent death of her husband had opened a door for Leeward and he had made the most of the opportunity by offering his help and attention to the young widow. Without anyone to manage the ranch it was only his bank's advances that had kept Kitty's ownership of the Cartright property in her own hands.

Leeward was in his thirty-eighth year and paid close attention to his appearance. He wore a sharp, neatly hand-tailored grey suit and his lank brown hair was cut and oiled on a regular basis. A gold watch chain hung across his matching vest and he had his ankle boots polished and shined fresh every day. A man of slight build with bland and unremarkable features, he had insinuated his way into the town with careful humility, impressing the locals with his generous donations towards many objects of civic pride. It was he who had funded the construction of the bell tower that now crested the inter-denominational chapel of prayer. A water wheel distributing river water to irrigate the farm fields alongside the flowing river had been his gift. He had even cleared and prepared the baseball playing field on vacant land to the east of the town. All of his actions had in this way encouraged a belief amongst the townsfolk of an upstanding and righteous citizen and subsequently many had been willing to make deals with such a trustworthy figure.

Thus he had acquired land and the ownership of property in and outside the town. Where his money came from was a mystery; some said he had struck lucky in the goldmines of the far north, others that he was the recipient of funds from deceased wealthy relatives. Whatever the gossip, there was no doubt amongst the population that he appeared to be an honest man; his whole demeanour and smart appearance had demonstrated this.

Right now, Leeward had achieved much of what he had desired on his arrival in Oakum but his secret ambitions were higher, one being the prospect of Kitty Cartright's hand in marriage. So far that had eluded him.

Kitty breezed in and he rushed to take her small handful of purchases from her.

'Here, Kitty, let me take those. You know I can always send one of the men to carry for you.'

She smiled in response. 'Now, Christopher, you must see that I have to do something for myself. You are too kind to me already as it is. Besides, some of those fellows are much too rough for my liking.'

Leeward looked at her benignly. 'I know, I do apologize for them. It is unfortunate, but they are a sad necessity in these trying times. Bank guards and cowhands are not company for someone as fine as you but better that than some ill befall you. You must see, it is your welfare only that concerns me.'

'I know, I know. You are truly a good friend, Christopher.'

He pulled out an office chair and held it for her. 'I would be more than just a friend, dear Kitty.'

Kitty straightened the folds of her black mourning-dress as

she seated herself, and she cocked an appraising eye at him. 'I am most grateful for your protestations of affection, Chris. But we have spoken of this many times before. I find my heart is still bound closely to poor Calum and until I shed that memory I cannot consider any alternative.'

Leeward sighed openly, 'As you wish, my dear. But please always remember that I am here, ready and willing to come to your aid in any way I might.'

He studied her profile as he spoke, taking in the lustrous sheen of her skin and the fullness of her proud figure. It was a treasure he would give a large part of his fortune to possess. Although he never demonstrated openly his lust for the woman, in the darkness of his mind he fevered for her and fantasized upon the day when she would be his. In part she already was; to his way of thinking it only waited for the sealing signature of a legal bond. But he was a man of cautious determination and it was his discipline in matters of courtesy that had won him so much of the town already. He could wait until Kitty was ready and willing but even so, secretly he hungered for the day when she would fall like a ripe fruit into his waiting grasp.

'You have heard of the man recently come to town?' he asked.

She shook her head negatively. 'No, I can't say that I have. Someone of interest?'

'He claims to have been a friend to poor Calum.'

'Really!' Kitty spun to look at him.

'Indeed, some of my cowhands came across him on the road up to the ranch. Apparently he has something of the roaming look about him. A grubby, drifting sort of fellow, probably well on his way elsewhere by now.'

'Maybe he has word of Calum's sad end. It would be a blessing to know such a thing. The War Department's telegram was such a poor missive with its limited information.'

'I doubt he could help, dear Kitty. In all probability he is some chancer hoping to make a few dollars on the back of such a claim. There are too many of these beggarly veterans wandering

28

loose at the moment.'

'But I should like to ask, Chris.'

'Well, it seems he has gone now. You must see, Kitty, the world is full of such men, that is why you need a protecting hand. I do fear for your innocence against such unpleasant trickery.'

Kitty laughed openly. 'Really, Christopher Leeward. You think I am such a wan creature who would faint away in a cloud of vapours at confrontation with such a creature. I assure you, Calum and I did not start our ranch without many hardships, all of which I shared. I can ride and shoot a rifle as good as any man should the need arise.'

'I know, I know,' he offered with a placating pat on her shoulder. 'I just cannot bring myself to consider such an image, though. To me you are solely an exquisite and esteemed example of superior female dignity and all that it enfolds.'

Internally, Kitty twisted uncomfortably at the platitudes. 'You set me on a pedestal, Christopher. I am no such thing, merely a widow woman making her way in the world.'

'Your modesty does you credit, Kitty, and there you have presentation of all that I say.'

'Tush! Dear friend. I will not have it. Now, I must be off,' she said, rising.

'Very well.' He offered her a small bow of repentance. 'I am wounded that I have offended you. Let me make it up. Will you dine with me tonight?'

She smiled. 'Very well, you flattering rogue. How can I resist?'

Kitty's curiosity was aroused though, and she took it in mind to ride out to the ranch and see that everything was well there. It had been many months since she had paid the place a visit and then it had been only to take her belongings away to the rooms that Leeward had arranged for her in town. The ranch still held too many sad memories for her. The sudden loss of Calum with no more than a brief notification of his death had remained a hollow place in her heart, and with no body to lay to rest the wound of his passing kept her grieving sadness open. For this reason she had avoided the place that held all her pleasant earlier memories.

With this in mind she made her way over to the livery stable to hire a trap and visit the ranch. As she approached the open doors of the stables she saw a broad-shouldered young man getting down from his horse. She recognized that he wore the saddle worn accoutrements of a Rough Rider and guessed that he was the man of whom Leeward had spoken.

She heard the man speaking to the stable hand, Jedediah Longstreet, an elderly hunchback who ran the place.

'I'll only be gone long enough to pick up supplies. Might need to hire a mule to backpack my goods though,' the stranger was saying. 'That a possibility?'

'Surely, mister,' answered Jed. 'Leave the mare here and take your time.'

'Might be you can help me on one other thing?'

'That so?' said Jed.

'Looking for a Mrs Kitty Cartright. Know where she might be?'

Jed looked over the man's shoulder and saw Kitty standing in the stable doorway. 'Look no further, young fella,' he said. 'She's standing right behind you.'

Jake spun around and saw the dark silhouette outlined against the sunlight of the street. He pulled off his hat and introduced himself.

'Name's Jake Rains, ma'am. Right pleased to meet you.'

Kitty moved into the interior and sunlight fell onto her features from the open rear of the stables. Jake could see that Calum had not misled him when he had described Kitty's beauty; her pale features and blond hair shone like a beacon against the blackness of her widow's weeds. Her eyes seemed to glow in the beam of light as she studied him, a blue like deep ocean water, eyes to drown in.

'Mr Rains,' Kitty nodded. 'I'm told you knew my husband.'

'That I did, m'am. We fought together. Became close pals

down there in Cuba.'

'You were with him when he died?'

Jake pressed his lips together at the memory. 'I was, m'am.'

Kitty looked down at her feet momentarily, then up again quickly. 'Perhaps this is not the place for such discussion, Mr Rains. But I should dearly like to know of his passing. Could you perhaps attend me in my parlour and give me some information?'

'Be glad to oblige,' said Jake.

'When would be convenient?' she asked.

'I have supplies to order but I'll be happy to visit when I'm done.'

'Thank you. I'm sure Mr Longstreet will direct you to my lodgings once you have concluded your shopping. I'm grateful and shall await your pleasure.'

Jake nodded. 'Think nothing of it, m'am.'

They went their separate ways. Jake crossed over to the store and placed his order for enough supplies to last a month. He was coming out of the store when he came across the slouching figure of Cole Reichter leaning idly against the wall outside on the boardwalk, as if he had been waiting there for him.

'You still here?' The dour cowboy commented as Jake passed.

'It appears so,' Jake answered, turning and staring the man down.

Reichter pushed himself away from the wall and closed with Jake, blocking his path. 'What's your game, cowboy?' he asked. 'You're up to no good here, I'll be bound.'

'If anybody's up to no good it's you, Reichter. Now stand aside before I knock you on your beam end. You are one ornery cuss, that's to be sure.'

Reichter squinted meanly and pushed back his campaign hat. 'Think you can that, do you? Like to see you try, you damned drifter. Just 'cos you're a military vet, don't mean squat to me. I made sergeant in my time and I seen plenty like you.'

Other passers-by on the boardwalk picked up the tone of their raised voices and began to back away. Men sitting on the bench outside the store were quickly on their feet and away, suddenly finding more important tasks to accomplish as the two men squared off.

Jake clenched his fists and stepped away a pace, ready to deliver the first blow if the cowboy made a move. 'Bet they busted you down more than they made you up,' growled Jake. Carefully he gauged the distance between them and watched Reichter's lip curl back as the man steeled himself to attack. The tenseness hung like a steel curtain between them. Reichter's frown furrowed into a deep cleft, a vein began pulsing on his temple. 'I'm gonna—' the opportunity to say more was stilled as a man in a neat suit stepped between them.

'What's going on here?' asked Leeward. 'You have a problem with this gentleman, Cole?'

Reichter faltered, blinked and backed off a step. 'Mr Leeward, sir. This here's that mean-sided drifter I told you about.'

Leeward pressed a restraining hand onto Reichter's chest. 'Now, now, Cole. There's no need for this attitude towards visitors to our town. Just because a body is a stranger it doesn't mean they necessarily mean us any harm. Now calm down.' Leeward turned to Jake and held out his hand. 'I must apologize, sir. The name's Christopher Leeward. I'm afraid Cole here can be a little over-protective sometimes.'

Jake took the proffered hand and introduced himself. 'Jake Rains.'

'Well, Mr Rains. I hope you will not think too badly of us here in Oakum; it's not our intention to be unwelcoming.' He turned back to Reichter. 'Now, Cole, you just get along back to the office. I'll be with you directly. Go on now, do like I say, get along.'

Reichter hooked the edges of his mouth down in the manner of a reprimanded child. 'OK, Mr Leeward. But I'm telling you. . . .'

Leeward gave him a warning look, 'That's enough, Cole. Do like I say.'

Reichter slouched off obediently with a quick hard glance over his shoulder at Jake.

'I must apologize again, Mr Rains,' said Leeward when the man had left. 'Cole is quick to anger, I fear. Though it's totally uncalled for behaviour in this instance. A rough fellow, but he does mean well, I assure you. Now, sir, allow me to offer any assistance I can during your stay. If he troubles you again, please let me know.'

'That's civil of you, sir,' said Jake, a little bemused by the turn of events. 'That fellow is certainly more prickly than a cactus pear.'

'Well, I'll have no more of it from the men in my employment. You can be sure on that score.'

'Everything all right here, Mr Leeward?' It was Sheriff Deeling who had come up behind, his coat drawn back, exposing his pistol.

'How do, Younghusband,' said Leeward, holding up a restraining hand. 'Everything's fine here. No trouble at all. A slight altercation with Cole Reichter, is all. But everything is settled amicably now.'

'Hurumph!' grunted the sheriff. 'Should keep that dog of yourn on a tighter leash, Mr Leeward.'

'I know it, I know it. But as I was just explaining to Mr Rains here, the fellow means well. Its just his way; a little uncouth I'm afraid.'

Sheriff Deeling gave Jake an appraising look. 'So you'll be staying around a while then, mister?'

'Could be,' supplied Jake.

'Well, I won't abide trouble here, you understand,' Deeling advised.

'Won't be me who starts any, Sheriff,' said Jake.

'Make sure it isn't. I run a clean town. Any trouble and I'll run you out on a rail.'

'I'm sure Mr Rains has no intention of anything like that,' Leeward put in.

With a quick warning look at Jake, Deeling flipped a forefinger at his hat brim and stepped away. 'Fair enough. Good day then, gentlemen.'

'There,' said Leeward. 'All settled. I'll be moving along also. Nice to meet you, Mr Rains. And remember, anything you need feel free to call on me.'

'I'll remember,' said Jake as he watched the man walk away.

Jake was certainly mystified by the attention his arrival in the town had created. As he made his way back to the livery stable he considered the problem and wondered at Cole Reichter's unwarranted antipathy towards him. Such things happened, of course, he recognized that. There were some people in the world whose meanness was as natural to them as breathing. Hard times forged hard people but even so he recognized that he would have to keep his wits about him when in the presence of the irate cowhand. If he did not he was sure it would end badly.

Jedediah Longstreet, the crooked-backed stablehand, allowed him a rented mule and was willing to arrange the packing of his supplies over at the store.

'Tell me,' asked Jake, 'you know if the army up at Fort Brill got any call for fresh saddle broke horses?'

'Sure do,' said the old man. 'They're always on the lookout for mounts. Why, you thinking on it?'

'Seems a good idea.'

'Reckon so,' agreed Jedediah. 'Could make a fair bit of ready cash in that line. Hard work though.'

'I ain't afraid of that.'

'Guess not.' Jedediah gave him a discerning look. 'Tell you what. We sometimes get a troop through here. I know some of them soldier boys right well. I'll get word to them if you want.'

'That would be fine by me. I'd be right grateful for any connections you got up there.'

'Fair enough, I'll do it.'

'Thanks, I'm obliged.'

Jake settled up with the old gent from his dwindling cash reserve and took directions to where Kitty's rooms were situated above the town bakery. On the corner of the block next to the bakery stood a small windowed shopfront that sported a neat handwritten sign: *Reading and Writing Lessons Weekly, Mail Read and Answered Saturdays. Mrs Katherine Cartright, prop.*

He climbed the wooden staircase to the first floor with the pleasant lingering scent of fresh bread still present in the air around him from the early baking. Before knocking on Kitty's door he took a look down at the town's main street and the steady flow of simple folk going about their business. Two young boys on bicycles raced past helter-skelter and a barrel-laden flatbed wagon hauled slowly along behind them, the driver calling out angrily as the boys skittered in front of his mule team. A stage from the stop-over was pulling out and a distressed clerk raced after it with a parcel of mail he had forgotten to place aboard. It was all a reassuring small-town picture and he felt as comfortable as he had when he first viewed the place from the valley heights above. For the first time in a long while Jake was encouraged to believe that at last he might have found a place where he could settle. His mood only darkened when he noticed Leeward and Reichter watching him through the window of Leeward's town office in the street opposite. Ignoring them, he turned and knocked on the door.

'Come on in, Mr Rains,' said Kitty, opening the door.

'Please, m'am. Call me Jake.'

'Surely. Will you take some refreshment?' she asked showing him into a well-appointed and neat parlour, with patterned wall-paper on the walls and heavy fringed drapes at the windows.

'I'm obliged, but no thanks, m'am. I'm fine just now.'

'Well, sit you down then.'

She seated herself opposite him and he could see by the way that the woman twisted a small handkerchief between her fingers that she was nervous.

'You teach some downstairs?' Jake asked, to put her at her ease.

'That's right.' She flashed a brief smile. 'There's quite a few folks as well as the youngsters that don't have their letters yet awhile, and until we get a schoolhouse and proper teacher I try to fill in. Saturdays when the stage gets in I usually read mail for parties that don't have the skill and then write out replies and such.'

Jake gave an approving nod.

'It's a small living,' she added.

They sat in silence for a moment, each waiting for the other to start.

At last Kitty drew a deep breath. 'So, you say you knew Calum?'

'I did that. We enlisted together. Became best friends along the way.'

'And how were things with him? I received very little post, you see,' she explained.

'Oh, he was fine. Just raring to go. We all were. It was kind of exciting then, at the start you understand, and sort of fun too. Volunteers from all over, from all kinds of backgrounds. Plenty of wild young buckaroos, it's true, but bold boys with spirit aplenty none the less.'

'And. . . ?' She paused and Jake could see she was struggling to hold back the tears. He realized there was no soft way of saying what he had to tell.

'It was before the San Juan Heights, m'am. That's where it happened. He took a bullet in the breast and passed soon after.'

A sob escaped Kitty. 'Oh, poor Calum.'

'He was a brave boy, Miss Kitty. He saved my hide a time or two, I can tell you. One time, I recall . . .' Jake hurried on, hoping to distract her from her tears. 'A Spanish sniper had me in his sights, I was trapped, crouching down behind a stump of tree with barely enough cover to hide my boots. Here comes Calum, reckless as rodeo roustabout, running through the

36

jungle hallooing like a wild thing. He's up there trying to catch that shooter's attention, draw his fire, you see. So I can mark his hiding-place and drop the fellow. And so it worked out. Calum was a bold and good friend.'

'I'm right glad to hear that, Jake. It does my heart good to know he stood his ground.'

'Have no doubts on that score, m'am. A more stand-up fellow I never met.'

Kitty wiped the tears from her cheek and Jake thought her glowing face and flushed lips a very pretty picture despite the task he was set upon. 'And did he say anything of me and our life here?' she asked.

'Sure did. Many times. He loved you well, m'am. And he loved the land you settled on; he spoke on it clear enough for me to picture it in my mind even though I had never been there.'

Kitty frowned at that. 'It is not so well now, Jake. I fear I could not manage things with Calum gone; the place has fallen into disrepair, I'm sorry to say. If it were not for the kind financial assistance of a good friend here in town it would be mine no longer.'

'Don't fret, Miss Kitty. Before he passed Calum made me promise on my oath to see you cared for and that place of yours set to rights. And that's what I aim to do.'

Kitty smiled despite her sadness. 'That is so kind, Jake. But I cannot expect that of you. I'm sure Calum had my best interests in his heart when he made you promise but have no fear, there is one here who will take things in hand, I'm sure.'

'Might I be so bold to ask who that may be?'

'Why, I don't mind at all, it is a Mr Leeward. An upstanding local figure and town benefactor.'

Jake looked a little askance and dropped his gaze to the floor. 'Just met the fellow, out there on the street.'

'Is that so?' she said. 'Well, he has often asked for my hand. A thing I could not offer until I had heard with certainty of Calum's passing, but now you have come to me with the news I am perhaps more able to look favourably on his offer.'

'Its not my place to say, I know that, m'am,' Jake fumbled with his hat, turning it by the brim in embarrassment, 'but perhaps it might be wise to hold off a spell. I am putting your land to order as I promised I would. I have a man with me and we have already begun the work. We shall have the place up and running within a six-month.'

Kitty's eyes opened wide in surprise. 'You will have. . . ? You have already started? What can you mean, sir?'

'It is under way,' Jake said eagerly. 'The roof is tiled and the wild growth cleared. We shall have corrals up soon. It is my intention to catch up wild mustangs and sell them to the army; that way we can fund all the repairs.'

'Why!' she gasped. 'You have taken my breath away. You have done all this without the asking?'

'I could not find you, Miss Kitty. It seemed best not to wait.'

'Well, I don't know,' she gasped, flustered. 'What a thing. It is most kind of you, Jake. But there is no need, I assure you. Whatever promise Calum enforced on you, I shall not hold you to it. Please, there is no need to take on such a momentous task.'

'I gave my word, Miss Kitty. And I intend to keep it. There's no more to say on it.'

She began to smile broadly, torn between annoyance and pleasure. 'You are certainly a dogmatic fellow, Jake Rains.'

'Can't say, m'am. I don't know what that word means, but I sure will do as I promised, come hell or high water, and that's a fact.'

Kitty pressed the fingers of both hands to her forehead. 'Let me think on it, I pray, Jake. This is a lot to take in all of a sudden.'

Jake clamped his jaw in determination, the muscles flexing on either side. 'Nothing to think on. It shall be done. I have a debt to pay here. A good friend saved my life more than once and only asked one single thing of me. He shall have all his acts of courage repaid.'

Kitty lowered her hands, pressing one against her heaving

bosom. 'You are certainly an unusual man, Jake Rains. To take on such an action for someone you barely know. Don't think I am not grateful. Not for one moment. But this cannot be. You must desist. Really. It is not possible.'

Jake suddenly got quickly to his feet. 'It has to be, and it will be, m'am. Now, I'll take my leave, with your permission. There's much to do.'

She opened her eyes wide in speechless submission. 'Is there nothing I can say?' she asked.

'No, m'am. I'll have you on your feet and back on your property with a six-month, that I promise.'

CHAPTER FOUR

'Why'd you haul me off him, Mr Leeward?' asked Reichter sulkily as they watched Jake enter Kitty's apartment.

'You are too hasty, Cole,' Leeward said slowly and thoughtfully. 'Much too hasty.'

Lorn Chaser sat silently on the edge of the office desk at the rear of the room and pared his finger nails with a sharp-pointed Bowie knife. He stole a glance at the two by the window, his face expressionless.

'I'll dry-gulch him, you just say the word. I'll nail his hide to a barn door,' hissed Reichter.

'We have things to maintain here, Cole. I want you to remember that. When the time is right I'll let you know.' Leeward kept his eyes fixed on Kitty's door, the skin on his face taut whilst his mind raced with jealous thoughts. 'It has taken me a long while to build all I have here. I will not see it brought down by any rash actions. It might be this Rains is no more than what he says he is, a messenger with word of Cartright's death. We must wait and see. So hold yourself in check.' He turned to fix Reichter with a hard stare. 'You understand me, Cole? You do anything without my word and it will go ill for you.'

Reichter was disconsolate and he turned to cast a look at Chaser in the shadows, looking to keep his standing with the other gunhand.

'You're the boss, Mr Leeward. I'll do as you say. Goes against the grain, though; I'll have you know that. I'm not the one to take anything from an uppity stranger.'

Leeward's face curled into a mean snarl and another, darker side of his outwardly urbane character was exposed. He whirled around and pushed his angry face into Reichter's. 'You think I give one good goddamn how you feel?' he fumed. 'You'll take my orders and like it or I'll have you spread-eagled on a five bar gate and a hot iron placed across your backside. You understand? Damn me if I won't do it myself. Hell's teeth! Why do I have such idiots in my employ?'

Reichter backed away nervously. 'No offence, Mr Leeward, I'm sure. I'm just saying you say the word and that drifter is buzzard meat, that's all.'

Chaser watched the interplay and allowed himself a slight smile as he bent his head and continued scraping at his nails.

Leeward took hold of himself, shaking as he calmed. 'Very well, Cole. Get along now, go on back to the ranch and stay there. On no account are you to run across that party's path.'

'As you say, sir. I'll do it.'

'Lorn, you go too. Make sure you keep this man in check, will you? I'm staying in town, I have an appointment later.'

Reichter hurried red-faced from the office with Chaser following at a more leisurely pace. Once they had gone Leeward stood at the window a long time, waiting impatiently for Jake to take his leave.

Leeward had made sure everything was prepared to his liking. The table was laid with a pressed and starched white dining cloth. A gleaming candelabra centred the table upon which polished silver utensils and imported Dutch china were laid out. A large vase of wild prairie flowers stood on an heavy sideboard and filled the room with their colour although a not altogether pleasant perfume. His small store room at the rear of the town office had been cleared especially, and he had gone to some lengths to make the room suitable to accept Kitty's presence.

41

Kitty smiled as she saw the room. 'Why, Christopher, how magnificent!' she exclaimed.

Leeward leant across the table and put a lighted match to the candles. 'You like it, my dear?'

'I certainly do. So civilized.'

'Well, we must bring some sort of decorum to our rough frontier existence occasionally. Please, sit yourself down. I'm having our meal brought in but I thought we might take a glass of wine beforehand.'

As Kitty seated herself at the table Leeward brought a decanter over from the sideboard and poured a ruby wine for her. 'Your health,' he said, raising his glass.

'Thank you for this,' she answered, lifting her own glass to his.

'So, Kitty, how was your visitor this afternoon? I couldn't help but notice Mr Rains climbing your staircase.'

'Oh,' she said, savouring the wine. 'Most affable. But very strange.'

'Strange? In what way?'

'Well, he is certainly a forthright fellow with an open and honest appearance. He told me all about Calum and their close friendship during the conflict. It appears that at the hour of his death Calum elicited a solemn promise from Mr Rains.'

Leeward seated himself and watched her features intently. 'A promise? What sort of promise?' he asked.

'Why, to restore the ranch and to take care of my well-being. Try as I might to reassure him that I had all the help I needed he would have none of it and insisted that he would fulfil his promise.'

Leeward set aside his glass and slid it across the tablecloth with his forefinger. He frowned thoughtfully. 'I venture that's a tad suspicious, don't you think?'

'I don't think he means harm, I must say. Apparently he has already started work clearing the place.'

Leeward started up. 'He is working on your property already without permission?'

'Indeed. Odd isn't it, but then, who am I to argue with such a generous offer?'

'Why really, Kitty,' Leeward exclaimed irritably. 'Can't you see the man is trying to insinuate himself onto the empty property. Once in he will make claim on it and it will take the devil himself to get the fellow off.'

Kitty shook her head. 'I don't believe it is like that, Christopher. I am sure he means well. There was no indication of anything underhand about the man. His sole aim appeared to be a fulfilment of Calum's last wish in repayment for the life-saving acts my husband performed on his behalf. Really, I don't believe there is any ulterior motive.'

Leeward shook his head sorrowfully. 'Oh, Kitty, Kitty, my dear. Your kindness does you credit but you are too easily taken advantage of. I fear for your generosity, I really do.'

'Well, I shall go and see what they are up to shortly, and if things are not going well I shall call on Sheriff Deeling to take the matter in hand.'

'They? You said 'they'.'

'Yes, he has another man working with him.'

'Do you know who this other fellow is?'

'No, I don't. Now, really Christopher, may we stop all the questions and enjoy our evening.'

Leeward drew a deep breath. 'Of course, my dear.' He turned and called to the back door. 'We are ready, you may serve now.'

The town eating-house had prepared the meal, and Sally, a buxom, well-intentioned serving-girl brought in a tray with bowls of vegetables and platefuls of steaming food. She eyed them both lovingly and laid the plates in front of the two with cheerful aplomb, wrinkling her nose cheekily. 'Will that be all?' she asked with a shy grin as if she were bringing in Cupid himself on a chafing dish.

'Rolls!' snapped Leeward. 'Where's the bread rolls, girl?'

The girl blushed awkwardly, 'Oh, yes. I forgot. I'll fetch 'em right off.'

Leeward was chewing his lip, his mind still coursing over the implications of Jake's invasion. 'Silly girl,' he growled.

'Now, now,' Kitty admonished him with an arched eyebrow and then turned to the girl. 'That's fine, Sally. This looks wonderful. Thank you so much.'

Sally sighed relief and almost curtsied as she took her leave. 'I'll fetch the bread. Sorry, m'am.'

Dolefully, Leeward hacked at his meat. 'Underdone, I told them medium rare, not raw.'

Kitty frowned. 'Why so distraught, Christopher? It is all well enough.'

'I apologize, my dear. It's just this affair with Rains; it concerns me.'

Kitty passed it off with a laugh. 'Do not distress yourself, I'm positive all will be well.'

'It had better be,' Leeward said with quiet venom, his eyes fixed on his knife as it sawed a pool of blood from the steak.

'You know,' said Kitty a little coyly after they had eaten for a while in silence. 'Now I am sure of Calum's passing and that he will never return to me. I am more inclined to look favourably on your earlier offer, Christopher. That is if it still stands.'

'Kitty!' Leeward smiled broadly, his demeanour instantly changing. 'Do you mean it? Oh, my dear, that would mean so much to me.'

'Well,' said Kitty, laying aside her knife and fork and giving a slight shrug. 'You have been so kind to me and I feel I must move away from the depressing notion of widowhood. It is surely a sad thing but I cannot, in all truth, commit myself to a lifetime dressed in black.'

Leeward got up from his seat and moved around to stand next to her. 'I do so agree,' he said 'You are much too young for such a thing.'

Quickly he grasped her hand in his and pressed his lips to it. 'It would be a completion I have much desired. To have you by my side would mean the world to me. Great things will be possible for the both of us together, I am sure of it.'

He knelt down suddenly, still holding her hand clasped firmly in his. 'Let me formally ask for your hand, dear Kitty. Will you marry me?'

As she looked into his eyes, a strange thread of doubt ran through her mind. Nothing she could quite place her finger on, only an indeterminate sliver of concern that caused her to hold back her answer for a moment. It was something she saw in his gaze. At first it appeared a joyful look filled with happiness and then a subtle shift took place, a shadow moved in, a darkness behind the apparent openness that turned his gaze into a gleam of inexplicable avarice.

'What say you?' he asked eagerly.

Kitty fumbled, bemused by what she had seen. She was saved by the return of Sally bearing a basket of bread rolls. 'Here we are,' the girl said, breezing in and pushing the door wide, her eyes widening as she saw Leeward's kneeling figure.

Leeward leapt to his feet in embarrassment. 'Don't you knock, girl?' he barked crossly.

'I beg pardon, Mr Leeward. I truly do.' The girl bit her lip, staring from one to the other in dismay. A faint smile began to play on her lips though, as she recognized what was taking place. 'Oh,' she said, lifting her hand to her lips. 'Oh, oh.' Sally recognized that romance was in the air and the simple girl was full of good will towards the pair. 'Does my heart good,' she said, cocking her head to one side wistfully.

'Dammit!' hissed Leeward in disgust, his features darkening and his earlier bad mood returning. 'Get out, you wretched girl.'

In that moment, Kitty saw with all clarity that she could never be Leeward's wife.

CHAPTER FIVE

'See 'em?' Sam asked, handing Jake the binoculars.

'Oho! A fine bunch. Twenty or so I'd say.'

He watched the mustangs roam slowly as they fed on the rolling grasslands at the foot of the mountains. The two men lay spread-eagled amongst brush on a hillock overlooking the herd. It had taken them a week of hard work, but now, back at the ranch a wide corral stood ready and waiting to accept the mustangs.

'How do you want to do this?' asked Sam.

'Wait a moment.' A movement had caught Jake's eye and as he watched he saw a stallion break free from a stand of trees. The heads of the herd turned to watch the proud animal as it moved amongst them. It was a handsome creature, a dappled grey, with a powerful body and good line. 'See that?' he said, handing back the binoculars. 'There's the leader.'

'Phew!' Sam whistled. 'What a critter. That is one fine piece of horseflesh.'

'Right enough. If we can get a rope on him the others will follow.'

'Let's do it. If we come on him from two sides, hang low in the saddle, look as if we are one of the herd . . . we're downwind here, so if we take it slow maybe we can get in close.'

Jake nodded agreement and without another word, they began to slide back down the hillock to where their ponies stood waiting out of sight. The two freed their lariats and mounted, moving off slowly in different directions. Hanging low, Indian fashion, along the sides of their mounts' necks, they approached the grazing animals. It was a gradual process and Jake kept his eye fixed on the stallion, watching for any sign of nervousness on the animal's part. So far the stallion had kept his head down, munching at the lush grass. They were within some 300 yards when the stallion raised his head and sniffed the air. The creature issued a soft whinny and pawed the ground. He sensed something but as yet could not place the danger.

Jake realized it would only be moments before their presence was recognized for what it was. He loosened the lariat, softly letting it trail out beside him, the loop held between his gloved fingers. Then with a frown of determination he pressed his heels into Penny's side and urged the mare into a leaping run. At that moment Sam followed his lead and the two charged towards the stallion at an angle to cut off its escape. The wild creature reared and snorted, shaking its head from side to side. The scent of man filled its nostrils and fearfully it took off at the run. Behind, the herd took fright at the sudden movement and swiftly followed their leader in a swirling rush.

With a wild cry Jake crouched forward, feeling the blast of passing wind as he raced on. He began to swing the lariat above his head in a tight circle. The stallion had a powerful turn of speed that almost left the two men standing, and he began to swing away from Jake, but then the animal saw Sam's approaching figure and changed direction back again. The zigzag lost the creature its advantage and Jake closed in to loop the lariat high in a swift cast that fell across the stallion's head. Still the animal sped on, its muscles bunched and gleaming in the sunlight. Jake was hard pressed to hold the stretched lariat as it spun out with a searing burn that he could feel through his leather gloves, and quickly he lashed it round his saddle horn. The stallion balked at the sudden restriction and Sam moved in to loop his own rope. He cast well and the stallion was held now from either side. It rose high on its rear legs, forelegs kicking uselessly at the tightening ropes.

'Come on!' called Jake. 'We'll lead him on a piece until he tires.'

The two men took the lead, keeping apart and leading the stallion between them as they made off fast in the direction of the ranch, with the herd following dumbly behind.

'Wahoo!' cried Sam exuberantly, a smile cracking his dust laden features. 'Don't this beat all.'

They ran in such a way, with the riderless stallion eventually striding out ahead and the two riders following behind on either side. Foam flecked from the horses' mouths and white bands of sweat arose on their heaving chests. It was then that the mulish Penny decided she had had more than enough and began to slow down with the obvious intention of giving up the chase. The drag pulled the stallion to one side, curving his path over towards Jake.

Jake feared there would either be a collision or the stallion would escape entirely. There was only one recourse. Kicking free of the stirrups as the two horses closed, he leapt across the intervening gap and landed astride the broad back of the stallion. With one hand he dug deep and grasped the flowing mane and with the other he wound the lariat around his wrist. 'Let him go!' he called to Sam. 'I'll ride him out.'

Released, the stallion surged forward and streamed away across the prairie, soon lengthening the distance between Sam and the following herd. Jake heard Sam call out but could not make out the words in the flying wind. He latched his thighs to the pounding ribs of the stallion and hung on tightly as the beast bucked sideways and skittered irritably until it continued on its wild ride.

The freed lariats flew out behind them, the ends whipping in the wind and cracking like thin snakes in the dust cloud that followed their passage. Jake cried out in exultation at the excitement of it all and sunk his fingers deeper into the thick mane, urging the animal on to even greater speed. He seemed to be flying across the prairie floor; never had he known such a powerful animal. He swore to himself that if he could hang on and bring the beast under his control he would never part with him, for he was a prince amongst stallions.

Two riders watched from a distance as the long ribbon of dust passed below them and raced away in a straight line like a steam-train on tracks.

'That's some kind of mustang Rain's caught hold of,' observed Buck Holdall to his companion Lorn Chaser.

'Sure is,' agreed the often silent Chaser.

Buck Holdall scratched his sideboards thoughtfully. 'Could raise a right fine remuda of cow ponies with such a stud, would-n't you say?'

Chaser nodded silently and with a parting glance the two wheeled their ponies and rode off.

It was an exhausted, begrimed and dust laden Jake Rains who rode slowly into the ranch late the following evening. The bucking ride had lasted all the first night and following day. They had covered an untold distance across the open prairie, and once the stallion had given in Jake had slept hunched over across the stallion's neck on their ambling ride back. His face was a white mask of dust and his eyes were red from the wind that had beaten him about during the run. Every bone in his body ached from the jolting and his fingers were stiff from the tight grip he had maintained throughout. The equally exhausted stallion had at last acceded to his commands and given in, and now Jake rode the final few steps towards the waiting corral where he could see that Sam had managed to bring in the rest of the herd.

He slipped from the stallion's back and freed it from the chafing grip of the lariats. Then with an affectionate pat on the neck he let the stallion loose into the corral. Tiredly, Jake went over to the trough and buried his face into the cool water. The shock revived him and he stood to strip off his shirt, then he worked the handle and pumped more water up into the trough. With a glug and a rattle a pulsing stream ran up from the well deep below and began to fill the trough. Jake shook off his gunbelt, boots and pants and sank his aching naked body into the cold water. He lay there with relief, allowing the sweat and dirt of the past days slough off him.

'Jake.' It was Sam, crossing over from the house.

'Howdy, Sam,' Jake croaked.

'See you did it, then.'

'Sure did. Rode me to hell and back though. That is some kind of animal, I tell you. Lord knows how far we went.'

'Well, partner, you'd better get decent. You near scared the daylights out of your visitor, coming in looking like a dust devil and then jumping buck naked into the water trough.'

Jake arched an eyebrow. 'We got a visitor?'

'Sure, the Widow Cartright's come calling. See how things were going.'

'Aw hell, pass me my pants, will you? I'd better go see her.'

Kitty sat waiting as Jake stomped, clothed but still dripping into the room. 'Sorry, m'am,' he muttered. 'Didn't see your trap there when I came in.'

'That's alright, Mr Rains. I just dropped by to see how things were.'

'Well, we been busy. Getting on with things.'

'So Sam has been showing me.'

'Coffee?' Sam asked, following Jake in and holding up the pot.

'Yes indeed,' Jake answered.

'A fine bunch of wild ponies you managed to bring in,' Kitty observed.

'The prize is that stallion though,' Jake said, slumping down into a chair. 'His bloodline must run clear back to some fine animal introduced by the Spaniards. Time he's finished with them mares out there we'll have the finest herd anywhere in the county.'

'So you still intend to breed horses and sell them on?'

'Sure do, m'am. That old barn out there needs some fixing, we need new tools and timber and that'll take cash money. Old Jed at the stables is letting me in on some contacts he has with the army. Tells me there's a ready market there up at the fort.'

'Please,' she said. 'As you've taken over my ranch and seem determined to set things right around here I think the least you can do is call me Kitty.'

Jake smiled tiredly. 'OK . . . Kitty.'

They looked at each other across the table, the last of the sun casting a long beam of orange glow into the room. Sam delivered Jake a tin mug of steaming coffee, his shadow flicking through the light as he made his way out of the door to give them some privacy. The sunlight mellowed Kitty's hair, glinting and turning her coils to bands of warm gold around her face. Jake felt his heart skip a beat as he watched her steady gaze.

'I'm obliged to you, Jake Rains,' she said quietly, her voice barely above a whisper. 'For all you've done.'

Jake nodded. 'I'll do what I said I would.'

'I can see that you will,' she agreed.

They stayed that way a moment, each looking into the other's eyes.

'I have some money set aside,' Kitty said. 'Some I've made from my reading classes and such. It's not much but it'll do as a stake to start things off.'

Jake shook his head. 'No need, Kitty. We'll get by.'

'This I insist on,' she said firmly. 'Sam tells me you've been footing the bill all the way so far and I cannot let that continue. I need to be a part of this too, Jake.'

Jake looked into the dark bottom of his coffee cup as he considered.

'Fair enough,' he agreed at last. 'We'll do as you say.'

'That's settled then. Now, I'd best be on my way before it gets full dark. You rest easy, Jake Rains. That was some ride you undertook.'

'You want Sam to accompany you back to town?'

'No, I'll be fine. I'll come by again soon.'

'Always welcome.'

CHAPTER SIX

The three men who rode into Oakum two days later were gaunt, hard-boned creatures. They wore stained broad-brimmed slouch hats, and homespun shirts under long-fringed greasy buckskin overshirts. Each carried a long-barrelled businesslike Sharps buffalo rifle, either in the crook of his arm or slung crosswise over his saddle bow. Pistols holstered on full cartridge belts hung at their waists and sheathed knives were couched into the belt straps. They rode silently, led by the tallest amongst them, all were bearded with long tangled hair that hung over their collars, but the leading rider's alone was crisped with a fur of white, like icy dew.

Leeward watched the three from his office window as they drew up and fastened their mounts to the hitching rail outside the Barrel of Beer. Lithely they slid from their mounts and stood for a moment, studying the street.

'Look like a cross 'tween dumb mountain men and stinking buffalo hunters,' observed Cole Reichter from behind.

'Look like men hard as hickory to me,' said Buck Holdall.

Leeward nodded, 'Think you're right there, Buck. Wonder what they're in Oakum for?'

'Probably drifting through,' said Reichter.

'Why don't you go over there and find out,' said Leeward in way of an order rather than query. 'Buck, slip along and let the sheriff know of our visitors.'

Inside the saloon the three wild-looking men stood drinking, an even space apart, their long rifles leaning against the bar beside them. Silently, they raised their glasses repeatedly, lowering the level in an open bottle with slow regularity as if answering a parching thirst. Reichter pushed open the saloon doors and ambled over, ordering a beer from the bartender. He stood for a moment watching the sombre trio, drew a long draught, wiped his lips on the back of his hand and set the glass down.

'Buy you fellows a drink?' he asked.

Three pairs of calm eyes turned to fix on Reichter. 'What d'ye say?' asked the oldest, a frown furrowing his creased brow.

'I said I'd buy you a round.'

'Why'd ye do that?'

Reichter shrugged, 'Just being neighbourly, you being new in town an' all.'

'No need,' said the oldest one, and the three pairs of eyes rotated to the front again.

'Name's Cole Reichter. Pleased to meet you.'

'That right,' said the oldest man without turning.

'How're you fellas called?'

The nearest, the smallest of the three, turned to face Reichter and answered slowly. 'We be the Macafees.' He kept his steady, expressionless gaze fixed on Reichter as if waiting for some sign of recognition.

'Well,' said Reichter. 'Pleasure to meet you all. You boys come far?'

'Some,' said the smallest man.

'Don't say much, do you?' Reichter huffed, getting slightly irritated.

'Not much to say,' answered the Macafee.

'Well, I don't know. Fellow's trying to be sociable is all.'

The eldest Macafee swallowed a glassful, then raised an arm, moving his smaller brother aside. He loomed over Reichter. 'We be lookin' for someone. A body name of Samuel Parks. You know him?'

Reichter felt intimidated by the stern character but his

normal bluster rose to the fore. 'Maybe I do and maybe I don't. What you want with him?'

'That'll be our concern. You know him or not?'

Reichter shrugged and went to turn away but a large bony hand shot out and grasped him tightly by the upper part of his gun arm.

'Simple question,' intoned the eldest Macafee.

'Hey, hey!' cut in the bewhiskered barman, bustling up to the bar. 'No trouble in here, if you please.' The middle Macafee raised a finger and pointed it warningly at the bar tender, stopping him in his tracks.

'Be still there, t'ain't no concern of yourn,' he growled.

'Leggo stranger, you're hurting me,' whined Reichter.

'Simple question,' repeated the elder, squeezing tighter. 'Samuel Parks, you know him?'

'Best you talk with Mr Leeward,' Reichter gasped in pain. 'He knows everybody around here.'

'That so? Then ye shall take us to him.'

And Reichter did as he was told.

The solemn trio stood in a silent line before Leeward, resting their hands on their upright rifle barrels. 'Gentlemen?' said Leeward.

'We be the Macafees,' said the eldest. 'Abraham be my given name, this one here be Ezekiel and the young one there Absalom. We done had a little baby brother too, name of Mose, but he's gone to the angels. Cut down by one Samuel Parks, a cursed murderer. We have a blood feud on that one now. Eye for an eye it says and so it shall be.'

'Sam Parks,' said Leeward thoughtfully. 'Can't say that I know this name right off. But what say we bring this before the sheriff? Might be he can settle the matter legally.'

Abraham Macafee shook his head. 'There can be no law involved in this other than the law of Jehovah. Only our hands shall strike down the offender. It is written and it is our right.'

'I see.' Leeward hummed. 'Well, allow me to ask about. If the fellow is in this county I will hear of it.'

The office door opened and Buck Holdall entered hurriedly with Sheriff Deeling in tow.

'What's this, Mr Leeward?' asked the sheriff, looking the three backwoodsmen up and down.

'Younghusband,' greeted Leeward. 'These three are the Macafee brothers and they are looking for a murderer who killed one of their own. Fellow by the name of Sam Parks. Do you have a wanted poster filed on such a party?'

Deeling pondered a moment, then shook his head slowly. 'Can't say I have.' He looked across at the three. 'The Macafee brothers, you say? Seems I recall that name from somewhere, though. You men been in trouble with the law before?'

'There is only one law we cleave to and that be the law of Jehovah, which is set above the rules of mortal men,' said the youngest, Absalom.

'Not around here, young fellow,' snapped Deeling. 'In this town, I hold court and you'll do as I say or I'll want to know the why of it.' His hand slid sideways to move away his drape jacket and expose the butt of his pistol.

In a swift movement, Abraham, the eldest, whipped his rifle butt upwards from off the floor, the gleaming wood ensconced in brass plate buried itself deep in the sheriff's stomach with a solid thump. With a groaning wheeze Sheriff Deeling folded over, his hands pressed together in his middle. Deeling made a continuing complaining noise much like an unoiled gate, until Abraham raised the Sharps in both hands and with a simple strong jab cracked the sheriff on the side of his head, stilling his noise and dropping him to the floor in a semiconscious faint.

'Whoa!' said Buck Holdall, jumping back a step as the sheriff almost fell on his feet. 'Steady there.'

The three Macafees raised their weapons to cover the room. 'Some has to be taught,' said the eldest Macafee hollowly, a pin-point gleam of penitential fire burning in his eye. 'Are there others here who would argue with the Word?'

'No, no,' said Leeward, raising both hands. 'We understand. Some things are unavoidable. Now, please, gentlemen. I am willing to help. Let me offer you accommodation at my ranch, the L double E, whilst I discover whether this Parks fellow is hereabouts. I tell you, I think I might know where he is but I must make sure.'

Abraham looked at him long and hard, then he turned to his middle brother and pointed down at the comatose sheriff. 'Ezekiel, take this one along to his own prison cell and lock him in.' He turned to face Leeward again. 'It shall be as ye say. We come to take a life but we shall take on the sustenance of life before all else. Cast your net wide, Brother Leeward, we know this dog be here somewhere. It will go well with you if ye find him.'

It only took Leeward one look into those burning eyes to know that the fellow and his kin alongside him were as crazy as a pack of rabid wolves.

'Cole,' he ordered. 'Take these boys out to the ranch. Set them up in the bunkhouse and see they are fed and well cared for.'

'Mr Leeward,' whispered Reichter. 'The hands in the bunkhouse won't like it. Y'know, sharing with these—'

'Do as I say, Cole,' whispered Leeward. 'Or perhaps you'd like to follow the sheriff's example. I'm sure Mr Macafee here would be glad to oblige.'

Reichter shuddered at that thought, 'Right. Yes, right, Mr Leeward, sir. Of course. Come along now, you Macafees, you just follow me.'

When they were gone Leeward turned to Buck Holdall. 'Go fetch Lorn Chaser, Buck. Stay here and hold yourselves ready. I have an inkling we might use these Macafees to do some work for us.'

Holdall gave him a calculating look. 'This wouldn't involve a certain Jake Rains now, would it?'

'Might well,' grinned Leeward slyly. 'Might just well do that.'

He took his hat from the stand then and without saying more went out, crossing Main Street and making his way over in a casual saunter towards Kitty's small office.

She sat behind her desk bent over a stack of unread mail.

'Good day, Christopher,' she greeted him airily as he entered.

Leeward swept off his hat. 'Kitty, you look as well as ever.'

She smiled at him. 'How can I help?'

'No way particularly. I just wondered how things were progressing at your ranch. Is all well there?'

'Indeed it is. Jake and Sam are working wonders. A new corral now with twenty mustangs that they are breaking in. The roof is fixed, corral's mended and undergrowth cleared, I must say they work like a pair of veritable Trojans.'

Leeward pushed aside an inkpot and seated himself on the edge of her desk. 'That's good news. "Sam" you mentioned, who is this Sam fellow?'

'Sam Parks. A man Jake has hired to help.'

Leeward registered the name and filed it away. He had noticed the familiar use of first names and it irked him to think of Kitty on such terms with the men, although he kept these thoughts well hidden.

'I heard they have a prize stallion out there. One of the boys saw it at full run out on the prairie. Looks to be a prime piece of horseflesh.'

'Yes indeed,' she agreed excitedly. 'We have plans to hold him back for breeding.'

'So you must be out there often. It seems I never see you these days.'

She kept her eyes down, concentrating on her mail. 'Yes, it is good to see the place alive again. I am there at work on a small vegetable garden.'

'So, perhaps you are planning on returning to the place permanently?'

She shrugged. 'Maybe. I don't see why not now that it is

habitable again?'

'Indeed, why not. But I miss your company, Kitty. And now we are promised in marriage, I think it were better that you were not out there alone and unaccompanied with those rough fellows. It could be a cause for gossip here in town.'

She raised her gaze slowly, chewing awkwardly on her lip. 'I have never confirmed my acceptance, Christopher. As you may remember?'

'But,' he said, getting quickly to his feet, 'surely, it was you who suggested it. You recall?'

'Perhaps,' she said doubtfully. 'I was a little rash. I am sorry, Christopher, if I misled you.'

Leeward coloured visibly, 'I am not misled, Kitty. It was agreed. As clear an agreement as one might expect; if that damned girl had not burst in I would have had it from your own lips. Even so, the matter was understood; surely you will not go back on your word now?'

'Oh, Christopher, please don't be angry. Let us be friends as we were.'

A coldness filled Leeward's face, 'Then you are now reneging on your earlier acceptance?'

'It cannot be, Christopher. I am sorry, it cannot be.' Tears were starting to form in her eyes at the distress she was obviously causing.

'No, no.' Leeward shook his head in a confused, disbelieving manner. 'You said you would look favourably on my offer. I have it all clear in my mind. There can be no other way, you must be my wife. The town . . . how will they look on me if you refuse now? I will appear a fool; that girl Sally will have told all. I will be thought a stupid, lovesick fool. It cannot be, Kitty.'

'I am sorry, Christopher.'

'Why? What is it? Something I have done? Or is it another, is there someone else? Is that it? One of those men? That Jake Rains? That's it; everything changed when he arrived. That is why you are out there so often. You have taken that common drifter as a lover. I shall see to him, I promise you; have no fear on that score.'

Kitty shook her head angrily. 'Good heavens, no, Christopher. How could you suggest such impropriety. Jake carries himself always in a most proper manner and Sam as well. Nothing of the sort would ever enter their minds. And it speaks ill of you that it should enter into yours.'

Leeward looked at her with disgust. 'You are such a fool, Kitty. You know nothing of the world or of men. Of course they think of you with only lust in their hearts and you in your innocence will only inflame them until something terrible happens.'

Kitty, her mood changing from contrition to one of anger, slapped down her open hand hard on the desktop. 'Stop! I will hear no more of this. Stop this instant. I see now that I saw truthfully into your heart that night, Christopher. It is you who harbours such ill thoughts, not Jake or Sam. Leave, please, I beg of you; leave this moment.'

Leeward's face showed only anger; there was no more of the calm façade he presented to the world; his features twisted into a taut mask of menace. When he spoke his voice held a flat, hard coldness.

'I will go, but be sure of one thing, Kitty. I shall rule this town and it will be me that says what is and what is not here. It is a certainty that you will come to me one way or the other, with your consent or without it. Consider this also, it is I that hold you to task. It was my bank that has lent you money. I can call in that loan at any time and foreclose, then what will you have? Think on that before you refuse me further.'

With that he turned, sharply slamming the door behind him so that the glass panes rattled in their frames. Kitty stared after him, her eyes full of shock and tears. She bit into her knuckles fearfully and then wept bitter tears.

It took Kitty an hour to recover herself, then she fetched the trap from the stables and drove at full speed out to the ranch. Jake and Sam were both there and had a whirling pony lashed around a post as they sought to throw a saddle across the animal. Jake had just managed to get the saddle on and was about to tighten the girth when he noticed Kitty drawing up in a clearly agitated manner.

'Something's wrong, Sam,' he said, jerking his head in Kitty's direction. 'Let this one go, we'd better see what's wrong.'

'You go,' said Sam. 'I'll deal with the bronc.'

Jake climbed over the corral rail and ran over to Kitty, who sat trembling on the trap seat, the reins still held limply in her hands.

'What's wrong, Kitty?' Jake took the reins from her hand and helped her down. 'You look white as a sheet, what happened?'

She leant against him gratefully. 'It was terrible. Mr Leeward . . . he was awful.' Her lips trembled; he could see she had been crying and was close to weeping again. 'He has threatened to foreclose on me if I do not consent to marry him.'

'Can he do that? Foreclose, I mean,' Jake asked.

'He can. His bank has advanced me the money to keep the property in my name.'

'No man can force marriage on you though, Kitty. That's not possible.'

She shook her head. 'It is difficult to explain. I thought of him all along as a kind friend and for a time I foolishly believed that we could make something of it. I admit I was tempted to accept his offer. Something held me back, though. He has been paying me such close attention ever since Calum left and has been very generous in many ways, but now I see his attentions were not founded on any true affection.'

'How so?'

'It is clear to me that he is all about acquisition, that seems to be his sole purpose in life. To own all he can. I fear he would take me as some kind of trophy – and the ranch property as well, merely to aggrandize his position and expand the empire he is building here in Oakum.'

Jake placed a protective arm around her shoulder. 'Well, it will not happen, Kitty. Don't you fret on it.'

She looked up at him gratefully. 'I thank God Calum sent you to me, Jake. Where would I be without you?'

'Come on into the house. Set a while and calm yourself. When you're ready, Sam and I will ride you back into town. We'll get your things and you can move back out here.'

Kitty sighed. 'It's true that I would prefer it that way now.' She paused. 'But it would start some awful gossip, I'm sure Christopher would see to that. Me being a widow alone out here with two bachelor men.'

'Don't think about it so, Kitty. Sam and I can move into the barn. Anyway, them townsfolk should be fretting more over the way Leeward behaves than the way you do. This is your place and you have every right to be here. We're just hands, same as at any other working ranch.'

She looked at him a while and gave a little smile. 'I think you are more than just ranch hands now.'

Jake caught her look and something mellowed behind his eyes; he was beginning to see Kitty as more than just his dead friend's wife and the remains of a promise to be kept.

'That's kind of you,' he said, as he led her into the house.

Later, as evening settled in, Jake and Sam saddled up and rode alongside Kitty's trap as they accompanied her back to town. Unknowing, they were closely watched from the cover of a pine grove by two riders hidden in the approaching gloom. Buck Holdall and Lorn Chaser moved slowly from the shadows when the trio were out of sight and rode down towards the deserted ranch house.

'What d'you say?' grinned Buck as they approached the rest-less mustangs in the corral.

'No problem,' answered Chaser, in his clipped way. 'Slicker than grease on a hot skillet.'

Jake and Sam sat waiting on the boardwalk outside whilst Kitty packed her belongings. It seemed to be taking her an interminably long time and Jake was getting restless.

'Been thinking, I've a mind to mosey on over to the sheriff's and fill him in on events,' he said to Sam.

Sam nodded. 'Might be wise. Don't think this matter will end here.'

'Come on then, let's do it.'

'You go ahead. I'll wait on Miss Kitty. Anyway, it's best I stay away from lawmen just now.'

Jake eyed him thoughtfully a moment. 'OK,' he agreed, deciding not to question Sam further on his mysterious aversion to the law. 'As you say.'

He got up and made his way along the quiet Main Street, alight with the soft glow from a few oil lamps set hanging outside storefronts and on sidewalk posts. The sheriff's office was dark and quiet as he opened the door to the shadowy room. Jake called out, 'You there, Sheriff Deeling?'

He heard a muffled reply coming from the cell area at the rear and he moved to the adjoining door.

'Who's that? You in here, Sheriff?'

The sheriff stood behind the bars of his own prison cell, a grim expression on his face and a trickle of dried blood on his bruised temple.

'What the hell's this?' asked Jake.

'Get me out of here,' snarled the sheriff. 'Some darned no-accounts rode in, busted me in the head and then threw me in here.'

Jake pulled at the cage door but found it locked. 'There's a spare key in my office desk. Go get it,' ordered Deeling. 'Leastways, there was if the critters haven't taken it.'

Jake fetched the key from the desk drawer. 'Who were they?' he asked unlocking the door.

'Three of them. Some kind of backwoodsmen. Called themselves the Macafee brothers. Right mean bunch.'

'They outlaws?' asked Jake as he helped the sheriff back into the office.

Deeling slumped stiffly down into his chair and began to fumble through his desk drawers looking for a set of wanted posters.

'Don't know right off,' he answered. 'But that name of theirs is ringing bells. There's some paper on them somewhere, I swear it.'

Jake poured water into a bowl and fetched a towel for the Sheriff.

'Here,' he said handing it over. 'There's blood on your head.'

Deeling gave up his search and wiped the wet towel over his face.

'Obliged. Head sure aches fit to bust.'

'These men still here?' asked Jake.

'Not sure. Last I saw of them they were over at Christopher Leeward's office.'

'Leeward, you say. They know him?'

'I don't think so. Not right off anyway. That man of his, Holdall, he come running to fetch me, says there's some strangers in town I should know about. Things got kind of tough and I ended up in here. In my own damned cell. I don't think I take too kindly to that.'

'Should say not,' agreed Jake. 'I come in here to advise you on Leeward's activities anyways.'

'You did?' Deeling looked up at Jake, holding the towel to his throbbing head.

'Seems he's been bothering Kitty Cartright, threatening to foreclose on her unless she steps up to the altar with him.'

Deeling's eyes widened. 'That a fact? Appears that old boy's getting a mite too big for his britches, don't it?'

'Well, seeing as he's the high honcho around here I thought it best you knew. Thing is, I'm pretty sure he won't let it end here.'

'OK.' Deeling sighed. 'I'll take it on advisement. I'm grateful for your help, son. Right now, guess I'd better take a turn around town see if these Macafee skunks are still around.'

'Sure you're up to it, Sheriff? You want some help?'

'No,' groaned Deeling, getting up stiffly and hoisting a double-barrelled down from the rack behind him. 'It's my job, I'll see it gets done.'

'You need it, just holler. Right now we're taking Miss Kitty back to the ranch for safe keeping.'

Deeling shucked shells into the shotgun. 'I'll come over and talk to her tomorrow. See if we can straighten out exactly what's going on.'

'Fair enough. Watch your back out there, Sheriff.'

'I intend to,' growled Deeling grimly, snapping the shotgun shut.

Sam was the first to notice that something was wrong. 'We've had company,' he said softly as they drew up outside the ranch house.

'Why'd you say that?' asked Jake, looking around.

Sam jerked his head over towards the darkened corral. The bar gate was open and the corral was empty. Jake urged Penny over and bent down over her neck to see if there were tracks. 'Damn it!' he growled. 'Can't see a darn thing.'

'What is it?' called Kitty from her seat on the trap.

'We've been rustled,' Jake answered. 'Stay where you are, Kitty. Sam, get inside and see if it's safe in there, then bring me a lantern, will you?'

'Surely.' Sam slid from the saddle and hoisted his six-shooter from its holster before opening the house door cautiously. 'It's OK in here. Come right on in, Miss Kitty.' He was back in a moment, a lighted lamp swinging in his hand.

'Sam,' said Jake as he dismounted, 'you're probably better at this than me; see if you can find sign here, will you?'

Sam knelt and studied the dusty ground around the corral gate as Jake crossed over and helped Kitty inside the house. 'Do you think its Indians?' she asked.

'No telling. Sam will know; we'll wait on him.'

'You hungry?' Kitty asked, noticing the frown on Jake's troubled face.

'Sure am.'

'Why don't you sit awhile and I'll rustle us up something. I brought some supplies with me out in the trap.'

Kitty rolled up her sleeves and began to stoke up the stove, rattling pots busily as Jake fetched the sack of foodstuffs from the trap.

'You remember where everything is?' Jake asked her.

She smiled across at him. 'Should do, I lived here long enough.'

Jake watched as she focused on her preparations, emptying butter, maize bread, ham and eggs from the sack. 'You can set the table if you like,' she said. 'Clean plates and cutlery and I'd like a cloth on that table there.'

'Yes, m'am.' Jake said, hunting for something suitable to use as a tablecloth; eventually he settled on a blanket as a last recourse. 'Looks like you're to home, Kitty.'

'Does me good to have people here,' she answered.

'You feel alright then? I mean, being here without Calum, an' all?'

She looked up for a moment, thoughtfully. 'I do actually. Strange isn't it? It's like turning a page in a book. A sad book, true enough, but a better page now, that's for sure.'

Jake slid the cork from a bottle of rye and poured two glasses. 'Here,' he said. 'This will settle you some.'

'Oh, no, thank you kindly,' she replied. 'I don't take strong liquors.'

'I think you could do with a little right now. For medicinal purposes. Look, I'll mix some water in, be a mite weaker.'

She shrugged and came over, a ladle in one hand and a pan in the other. Setting down the pan she took the offered glass and sniffed at it tentatively before venturing a sip.

'Gah! It tastes awful. How can you drink that stuff?'

Arching an eyebrow, Jake tossed back his own drink and

quickly poured himself another. 'Practice,' he said.

'Hey,' said Sam coming in the door. 'Save some of that for a working man, will you?'

'So?' asked Jake as he poured. 'What's the story?'

'There were two of them. Two shod ponies. The rest of the herd lit out in all directions, them not being shod yet awhile made it clear. The two horse-thieves went off in a direct line east, dragging one unshod mustang behind. We can guess which one it was.'

'They've got the stallion,' Kitty said, stating the obvious for them all.

'What lies east of here?' Jake asked her.

Kitty looked at him ruefully. 'That'd be the L double E, Christopher Leeward's place.'

'Should've known,' grunted Sam. 'Plain as day, that'll be where the mustang is.'

Jake frowned. 'Maybe, maybe not. We have to be sure.'

'He's just out to rile you,' Sam observed. 'Looking to stretch you some, hoping you'll come all fired up so he and his gunmen can cut you down.'

'I know it,' agreed Jake. 'So, here's how it is, Sam. This ain't your fight. No hard feelings if you feel the need to move on. I've got to stay. Gave my word on that.'

Kitty turned irritably, an exasperated tone in her voice.

'Now listen up you two. There's absolutely no necessity for this, it's not worth dying for. None of it is.'

Sam kept his eyes fixed on Jake. Slowly he sipped his whiskey then gently set down the glass. 'Obliged for your consideration, Jake. But I think maybe I'll stick around awhile.'

Jake nodded a grateful acceptance. 'Well then, when we've got some daylight we'll catch up the herd without a leader. They can't have gone far, but first we'll make sure on that stallion; he's our bank money. Right now though, let's eat. It's been a long day.'

CHAPTER SEVEN

A crisp early morning, with a bright sun creeping up over the horizon and blowing a blaze of white light across the countryside to greet them. Jake squinted into the sunlight, then turned to Sam. 'You ready?'

'As I'll ever be.'

'Then let's go.' He turned Penny over towards Kitty, where she stood waiting at the ranch house door.

'Will you be alright on your own?' Jake asked.

Kitty picked up the Winchester leaning against the doorpost and cranked a shell under the firing pin with practised ease.

'I'll be just fine,' she assured him. 'You two take good care of yourselves, you hear?'

'Don't worry. We'll be back safe soon enough.'

'Make sure you are, Jake Rains. I'll hold you to that.' Their eyes met and Jake could see the worry and concern she held for him in her gaze. It surprised him a little and he felt a sudden warmth flow through him. He tipped his hat and nudged Penny on.

They rode for a good hour across the prairie grasslands towards the rising sun. Sam slowly tracked the overnight trail that stood out clear in the slanting sunlight and led them deep into L double E land. The countryside rolled through soft grassy hills with sweeps of blue spruce and jack pine running across their path and as they picked their way through a hillcrest copse,

Jake suddenly called for a halt.

'I smell pig slurry,' he said, sniffing the soft breeze blowing towards them.

'Uhuh,' agreed Sam. 'The ranch must be up ahead, over the hill.'

They dismounted, tied the animals and, taking their rifles, made their way on foot through the trees. Pine needles crackled underfoot and the fresh smell of the pine was offset by the farm-yard stink from below. Scrub bush marked the crest edge, where they crouched down amongst the undergrowth and peered into the valley below.

The ranch was a large settlement of timber buildings and corrals surrounded by flat open country. The main house, a long, low building constructed of stone stood central to the rest. The place spoke of a wealthy establishment, with plenty of room for hired hands and livestock. Stabled ponies whinnied from a large stable barn and smoke rose from a cookhouse set to one side of the main house.

'They're up and about,' Sam observed quietly as he watched a solitary cowhand in his long johns make his way past the pig pen towards a privy outhouse, causing a flurry of chickens to run before him as he went.

'You see the bait?' asked Jake indicating a large corral fronting the house. The stallion, the only horse in the corral, turned its head in their direction and scented the air, pawing the dust as it did so.

'Yep, they laid him out all ready for us. That old pony knows we're here, though,' said Sam.

Jake grunted. 'Let's hope nobody else does.'

Sam nestled down deeper amongst the scrub. 'So what do you reckon?'

Jake rubbed his jaw thoughtfully. 'Two ways. We either go in there and face them down or wait until nightfall and sneak in.'

Sam harrumphed. 'Big choice. You seen the size of that bunkhouse? If it's full they got a parcel of manpower down there. We go in bold they're going to chop us down easy. I favour a night visit myself.'

'Maybe,' Jake accepted dolefully. 'Just would like to see that Leeward face to face one time.'

'Doubtless you'll get the opportunity soon enough.'

It was then that Jake felt the cold hard muzzle of a rifle barrel press deep into his cheek.

'Been waiting on thee,' said Abraham Macafee quietly.

Jake and Sam spun around to see the three buckskin-clad figures standing over them, long rifles cocked and ready. They had appeared as silently as ghosts and looked just as grim.

'Macafee!' spat Sam in surprised recognition.

'Truly, Brother Samuel. We are here and we have you fast, all as the Good Lord intended. Now, shed the hardware.'

Jake looked across at Sam, 'You know these back-jumpers?'

Abraham's rifle butt swung across and caught Jake a warning clout high on the cheek. 'Say nothing unless it is asked of ye. Now, do as I say and lose your weapons.'

Jake rubbed his jaw and with a resentful look slowly obeyed the eldest Macafee.

'It is the Lord's vengeance alright, Brother Abe,' chuckled the youngest Macafee, watching the two prisoners unbuckle. 'They came like lambs to the slaughter.'

'Could it be otherwise, Absalom? We have the right on our side and Samuel Parks shall pay for his bloody murder. Oh yes,' he stared down hard at Sam. 'Ye shall atone, sinner.'

'Mose came for me and you all know how it was,' protested Sam. 'I had no choice. None at all. It was him or me.'

Abraham fumed slowly, the Sharps shaking in his hand as his anger rose. 'Mose was a sweet child. There had to be provocation. He was tender in his years and you gutted him like a river fish.'

'He was woman beater,' spat Sam. 'Near beat that poor saloon gal half to death, then took after her with a knife.'

'She was a harlot!' roared Abraham, his bellowing voice

69

echoing amongst the trees and startling the birdlife, which fluttered wildly. 'Better dead than soil men with her sin.'

'Well, young Mose didn't seem to mind the soiling,' snapped Sam. 'He was with that popsy for a good hour before he started beating on her.'

Abraham leant down, so his face was close to Sam's. His voice lowered to a deep threat as he slid a broad-bladed Bowie knife from his belt.

'With this very blade thee did the deed, Samuel Parks. A sword of righteousness it shall be now and with it ye shall repay the debt.'

'Can we do it now, Brother?' sniggered Absalom, a shiver of mad excitement trembling through him.

Abraham straightened and glanced across at Ezekiel, the middle Macafee. 'What say you, Ezekiel?'

This solemn Macafee, the most silent of the three, looked down at the two prisoners where they crouched. 'I say we make example of them both.'

'Wait!' cut in Sam. 'This here is Jake Rains, he has nothing to do with any of this. He should be set free to go his way.'

'He rides with thee, does he not?' intoned Ezekiel. 'Then he is tarred with the same brush. Murderers two, I say.'

'Stand ye up with your hands held high,' growled Abraham. 'Example it is. Go then before us, down into the valley. Let us show those lowly heathens down there how the Macafee skin their catch.'

Hands raised, Jake and Sam stumbled out of the scrub bush and side by side made their way through the waist-high grass that covered the hillside. The three brothers spread out and followed, their long rifles held ready.

'What's this about?' asked Jake.

'You heard it back there. Their youngest brother was even crazier than the rest of them. Ran into him in a drinking house down on the Powder River. Kid was demented as a drunk loon, he took to hurting the girl and I stepped in to stop it. So he went for me and I had to use his own knife on him. Say, look here, I'm real sorry to get you into this, Jake.'

'You said you had troubles. I was warned.'

'Sure, but the Macafees have an awful bad name. They do things their own way without a tinker's cuss for the right or wrong of it. Just get themselves fired up on the Good Book in all its literal form and go out killing and burning as if they were God's own avenging angels.'

'Bad they are, these are the three that beat up on Sheriff Deeling and locked him in his own jail. White men behaving worse than Apache savages, that ain't right?'

'That's the truth. At the time back then it seemed best I light out rather than front all three of them together, but they've damned well tracked me all the way out here.'

'Could be they had a little help finding you,' Jake said, nodding towards the stallion in the corral.

'You think Leeward set this up?'

'That's my guess. Getting these Macafees to do his dirty work for him.'

The valley slope levelled out as they approached the ranch and at their arrival curious hands began to wander out of the bunkhouse on their way to breakfast. They formed a wide semi-circle of yawning and stretching onlookers as the five trudged in.

'Whats this, Macafee?' called one. 'Caught you some rustlin' types there?'

'Stand aside,' called Abraham. 'These be murderers here and shall face the justice of the Lord delivered by my hand.'

'What you aim to do, Macafee?'

Abraham ignored their further questions and nudged Jake and Sam over towards the high arched timber entrance to the corral. 'Get me some rope,' he called to his brothers.

Lariats were fetched and Jake and Sam had their wrists lashed together before them whilst the free rope ends were tossed high over the gate arch. With a jerk, Ezekiel and Absalom tightened the ropes and began to pull them in, raising Jake and Sam up on

71

tiptoe. Young Absalom began to giggle nervously, his eyes wide in his head.

'Up there, lift them from the ground,' ordered Abraham, sliding the broad bladed knife from its scabbard. 'See this, Samuel Parks. First I shall skin your hide before I slay thee.'

Jake and Sam were lifted until they dangled free of the ground, their bindings were fastened off and Absalom and Ezekiel ran around to face the two swinging men. Abraham stood before them, then swung his blade in a threatening arc that caught the morning sun in a glittering flash of light.

'Hold on now,' a voice called from the restless crowd of cowhands who, despite their rough lifestyle, were beginning to take an uncomfortable objection at the way things were going. 'This ain't the way things is done. These men got to have fair trial.'

A mumbled chorus of agreement followed.

'You men stand back unless ye wish to join them!' Abraham ordered hoarsely. 'This is family business we talk of here and the settling shall be ours alone.'

Absalom suddenly started forward, wildly pointing an accusing finger at Sam. 'See, see!' he screamed in a voice high with mania, 'Just see what happens now. Thy judgment is come, Samuel Parks.'

In stepping forward in such a way, he accidentally saved his elder brother's life. The shotgun blast that was intended for the knife-wielding Abraham caught Absalom in the side under his raised arm and threw his torn body hard against his brother who stumbled and fell under the weight.

'Don't no one move!' ordered Sheriff Deeling in a loud voice as he stepped out from the cover of the bunkhouse, the smoking shotgun steady in his hand. 'I got another barrelful here for any that wants it.'

Ezekiel ignored him and ran swiftly for the Sharps rifle he had left propped against the corral bars. Deeling did not hesitate; he fired again and a plume of dust sprang up around Ezekiel's running feet. The twelve-gauge shot swept his legs from under him as he tumbled with a scream to the ground.

Abraham pushed aside Absalom's limp body and rose quickly to his feet. He moved lithely, like a mountain cat, far more smoothly than one would surmise possible for a man his size and age. With a wild look of rage he ran towards Deeling, the Bowie knife still clasped in his fist. The sheriff dropped the empty shotgun and, sweeping back his coat tails, drew the Scholfield holstered there. It was a practised draw, slickly enacted with the hammer cocked ready as the draw was made. In a split second Abraham was looking down the dark barrel of the levelled pistol. He skidded to a halt, crouching, his hair blowing wildly as he stared at Deeling with red-rimmed eyes. 'My brother is dead,' he snarled, baring a clenched row of unhealthy looking teeth.

'You want to join him?' Deeling answered calmly. 'Then just come ahead. If not, then drop that blade.'

Abraham twisted with indecision, his head swinging angrily from side to side, until he finally threw the knife aside in disgust. Slowly he raised himself to his full height and glowered at the sheriff.

'Raise your hands over your head,' Deeling ordered.

Brow furrowed, Abraham just stood there, his chest heaving, never taking his eyes from the sheriff.

'Fair enough,' said Deeling, firing a warning shot that spouted dust from between Abraham's boots. Slowly the big man raised his hands, the hate exuding from him as an almost tangible vibration that filled the space between the two men.

'You men,' Deeling ordered. 'Cut down those two.'

Cowhands ran forward obediently and Jake and Sam fell to the ground as the ropes were cut. They jumped up, hurriedly pulled the lashings from their wrists.

'You came just right, Sheriff,' Jake called.

'I know it,' said Deeling. 'Was out to your place to see the widow Cartright and she told me what was up. Took out after you and got here when I did.'

Rubbing their wrists, Jake and Sam picked up the discarded Sharps, then Jake crossed over to Ezekiel, who was lying squirming silently on the ground clutching his wounded legs.

He looked up as Jake knelt and took the knife and pistol from his belt. 'See to my baby brother,' Ezekiel begged through gritted teeth.

'Your baby brother's a dead man,' said Jake with some satisfaction. 'And those legs of yours are peppered real fine. Going to be a mite of trouble picking that lead out of there.' Jake looked around at the watching cowhands. 'You men best take him in the house, see if you can get him bandaged up. Is Leeward here?'

The men moved obediently forward to pick up Ezekiel. 'He's in Oakum town with his crew, I guess. Ain't been here a spell,' a small, square-faced, clean-shaven cowpoke answered.

'Well,' said Jake, 'that there stallion in the corral is mine and I intend to take him with me. You hear that, Sheriff? They come took this horse and scattered the rest of my mustangs last night. That's what brought us out here.'

'I hear you, Jake. If he's yours then you take him. First though, one of you come on over here and bind up this big dumb ox for me, will you? I got to keep him under the gun.'

Abraham hissed malevolently as Sam approached him, lariat in hand. 'Touch me if you dare, you sack of sin.'

'Aw, hell,' muttered Sam tiredly. He swung a mighty uppercut from low on his waist. The blow caught the tall Macafee right on target under his bearded jaw. Abraham went over as if he had been pole-axed; like a felled tree he dropped straight down and lay still on the ground.

'That'll do it, mister,' chuckled Deeling, holstering his pistol. 'Liked to have had a shot at that myself, all said and done.'

Sam volunteered to ride shotgun and help the sheriff take his prisoners back into town. A teamed flatbed was provided to carry the wounded Ezekiel, dead Absalom and a trussed Abraham sitting upright beside them.

Meanwhile, Jake fetched their tethered horses and firearms from up on the hill and roped up the stallion with the help of the small, square-faced cowboy who appeared to be the most accommodating of the cowhands.

'You see who brought him in?' asked Jake as they put a halter on the stallion.

The cowboy looked cautiously over his shoulder at his companions, who, now the fun was over, were making their way back to the bunkhouse.

'Listen, mister. I've had it with this place. I don't like what goes on here and I'm aiming to quit. So it don't matter much what I tell you. It was Buck Holdall and Lorn Chaser that came in late with the stallion.'

'I'm obliged for your honesty but you know that that there is horse-stealing by those two. You willing to bear witness on it?'

The cowboy shook his head and answered awkwardly. 'Sorry, I fancy my life too much for that. Leeward and his buddies would rub me out before it even got to trial.'

'What's your name, fella?'

'Clay Rudebaugh.'

'Well, thanks for your help anyway, Clay.'

Clay looked at Jake for a moment, chewing his lip with indecision. He had bright-blue eyes in an open face that gave him an almost childlike appearance despite his rugged features.

'Look, mister. Like I say, I want out of here. Any chance of work at your place?'

Jake studied the blocky figure, whose compact physique fitted into no more than four and a half feet of stature. Jake could see by the hardness of the man's hands that he was not afraid of work.

'Could be. I don't own the place but if you've a mind you could tag along and we'll see what the owner says.'

Clay grinned. 'I'll do it. Can you wait whilst I get my possibles?'

'Surely. You have pay coming here?'

75

'That's all right, I can come by later for it.'

Jake nodded. 'Go get your stuff and I'll meet you up on the hill there.'

With a wave of farewell he set off for the stand of pine above whilst Sam and the sheriff took the wagon road back to Oakum.

In all Jake considered they had been very lucky. He was still a little unsure about Clay Rudebaugh though, but he knew they would need help gathering up the mustangs and breaking them ready for riding. If the man was capable it would certainly bring a payment from the army closer and they needed the money if he was to bring the ranch up to standard.

Jake gave the stallion the once over whilst he waited for Rudebaugh and was pleased to find that the animal looked in perfect condition. The stallion was a proud beast and stood stock still, only trembling slightly during Jake's examination. Jake stroked his neck and spoke softly to calm the animal, who watched him carefully from the corner of his eye. The tensile strength under his touch felt to Jake as if the animal could fly if given half the chance.

'You certainly are a handsome one, that's a certainty,' Jake whispered. 'What are we going to call you now, I wonder? Something fitting for such a fine animal.' His hand slid along the sleek flanks and he patted the horse's rump affectionately. 'How about "Prince"? Because that's what you are. Right royal, out in front of the whole herd.' The stallion turned to look at Jake and gave a soft whicker as if in recognition of the name. 'OK, so Prince it is.'

Clay Rudebaugh came up the hill riding a pinto cowpony and pulled up alongside. 'Here I am, Mr Rains. Ready and set.'

'Call me Jake,' said Jake as he mounted up on Penny.

'That stallion there was certainly worth the trouble,' observed Clay.

'Sure was, he'll be our stud.'

'Then you'll be ranching ponies rather than cattle?' Clay asked as they set off.

'Well,' said Jake. 'There's a lot of wild mustang over by the mountains, so it might well be that way.'

'Then you'll be pleased to hear that there ain't a wild one that I can't handle.'

Jake grinned at the little man's confidence. 'You'll sure get your chance to prove that.'

On the ride back to town, Sam could feel the venom being sent his way from Abraham Macafee as if it were a veritable electric cloud. He avoided looking at the backwoodsman but kept his rifle laid in readiness across his saddle horn throughout the whole trip. Abraham muttered vile threats aimed at Sam, and occasionally his brother could not keep back a groan of pain from his torn legs as the wagon jolted over ruts in the road.

Sheriff Deeling kept his eyes straight ahead ignoring the ramblings from the two men in the back.

'You're Sam Parks, right?' he asked eventually.

Sam nodded.

'Where you from, Mr Parks?'

'Well, I get around. All over, I guess,' Sam answered vaguely.

'You're with Jake Rains at the Cartright place right now?'

'That's it,' agreed Sam.

'You know him from Cuba?'

'No, never did sign up for that one. How about you, Sheriff?' Sam said, seeking to divert the subject away from himself. 'You pulled on that hog leg back there like you knew what you were doing.'

Deeling allowed himself a casual grin. 'Like you, son. I've been around.'

'Old time lawman, huh?'

'Some. Stood with the Earps awhile. Backed up Hickok once and deputied Bat Masterson in the bad old days.'

'Don't know if they're any better days now,' Sam said, thumbing the two prisoners on the wagon bed.

'Well,' sighed Deeling as they rolled into the approaches to

Oakum. 'We're getting there. Slow but sure, we're getting there.'

Chris Leeward watched the wagon from his office window as it pulled up first at the undertaker's and then made its way over to the jailhouse.

'Looks like the Macafees messed up,' observed Buck Holdall, standing beside him.

Leeward's face tightened. 'Appears we're going to have to take some drastic measures to keep this town.'

'Yeah. What're you planning on doing?' asked Cole Reichter from the rear of the room.

'I'm thinking on it,' murmured Leeward.

'Whatever it is, I'm ready for it.' Reichter grinned. 'I do love raising some hell, that's for sure.'

Sam helped the sheriff place the two miscreants in the jail cell and asked if Deeling needed any more help.

'No, that's it. I'll get the doc look at the hurt one and then we just wait for the circuit judge to come by. Reckon these two mad dogs are bound for the penitentiary as it is.'

'Well, if that's it I'll head back. Jake's going to need help catching up those mustangs.'

'Obliged for your time, Mr Parks.'

'Guess we owe you that one, Sheriff. If you hadn't turned up when you did we'd be dead meat by now.'

'Well, if you find out exactly who did take that stallion let me know. That'll be a rustling charge and I'll bring in whoever's responsible. Just don't go taking the law into your own hands, you hear?'

Sam nodded, tipped his hat and left.

Deeling watched thoughtfully as Sam rode away down the main street. He went over to his desk and began ferreting around amongst the piles of wanted posters he kept in a drawer there. There was something about Sam Parks that nagged at him and his naturally suspicious mind suspected that somewhere the cowboy had a history that he did not want uncovered.

Kitty was washing clothes when Jake got back. She was out by the water trough, a big zinc tub beside her with a washboard at one end. She wore an old apron, her sleeves were rolled up and her hair was undone and tangled around her forehead. No more the neat reader of letters, she now looked more like a sodbuster's wife, and Jake smiled to see her so. He was pleased to notice though that she had kept the Winchester propped up within easy reach. Kitty was hanging the wet clothes over the empty corral posts when the two men came in sight; quickly she picked up the rifle and, holding one bubble-covered wrist up to shade her eyes, she squinted at the new arrivals.

'Glad to see you safe, Jake,' she called, lowering the rifle. 'And with the stallion too.'

'He has a name now. We'll call him Prince.'

She laid aside the rifle and studied Jake's companion. 'And who's this with you?'

'Name's Clay Rudebaugh, m'am,' the cowboy introduced himself, sweeping off his hat in greeting.

'Clay's looking for work. Says he's a good hand with horses,' offered Jake.

'Well, as long as he doesn't mind no more than food and a barn bed until we make some money, he's welcome.'

'I explained it all on the way over and Clay's willing to go along with us until we sell the herd,' said Jake.

'Fine.' Kitty smiled. 'We can do with all the help we can get. Come on inside when you're ready, there's fresh coffee brewing.'

Jake led Prince to the corral and set him free. The stallion pranced and skittered around the corral for a while before settling down. 'He's beautiful, Jake,' Kitty concluded.

'Sure is,' agreed Jake contentedly. 'We'll have a princely line out of him all right.'

Clay took their horses and unsaddled them, letting them drink from the trough.

'Best bring your wash in, m'am,' he said, with a shy grin. 'That critter'd like nothing better than to chew on them bloomers you leave 'em hanging there.'

Kitty blushed and hurriedly gathered in her underwear. 'I'll get a proper washline fixed up for you,' Jake said, smiling. He helped her carry the wet clothes inside and they set them down on the table.

'How did it go?' asked Kitty.

'Pretty rough. We were saved by old Sheriff Deeling, who came along at just the right moment.'

'He sure set off at a pace after he came here.'

'Well, I'm right glad he did. Sam's helping him take some no accounts back to the town jail right now.'

'Was it Christopher Leeward and his cronies?' Kitty asked tentatively.

'No, he wasn't there. Just the ranch hands and some ornery backwoodsmen who had an old bone to pick with Sam.'

'Is he alright?'

Jake nodded. 'Sam's just fine. Should be along directly, then we'll go get those mustangs. It was Leeward's men, though, that took the stallion and bolted the herd.'

'Really!' Kitty frowned crossly. 'Why would they do that?'

'Get under our skin, I guess. And set up the scene so we'd walk into those crazy backwoodsmen. Must say, the fellow's beginning to irritate me some.'

'Well, be careful, Jake. I don't think it will be wise to cross him.'

Jake shrugged. 'Could say the same about me. But if he leaves us alone I'll keep clear of him.'

CHAPTER EIGHT

It took them a month of hard work but by the end of it they had a workable bunch of mustang remounts to trade at the fort. Clay managed to fit in well with the other two men and they all got along as a companionable team. The little man was as good as his word and he stuck to the bucking broncs as if he were glued there, breaking in twice as many as Jake and Sam did put together.

Kitty avoided the town and it was Jake or Sam who picked up supplies every so often. There were no more run-ins with the Leeward crew and everything seemed to have settled into a peaceful train.

It was on such a supply trip that Jake dropped by the sheriff's office to find that he still had the two Macafees imprisoned there awaiting trial.

'Found old paper on them. I knew I'd seen the name somewhere before,' Deeling advised Jake. 'Appears they're wanted to answer some matter concerning a travelling snake-oil man over in Oklahoma. Apparently the fellow made complaint against the brothers after they beat him bad. He was trying to foist a cure-all medicament he claimed was a miraculous oil from the Holy Land on the local population. Promised it was the same embalming fluid that they used on Jesus after the crucifixion. Seems this offended the Macafees over-zealous religious notions and they set about him.'

Jake glanced over at the closed door to the cells from where came the sounds of distant mumblings.

'That going to stick in court?' he asked.

'I doubt it. The shuckster's probably long gone by now,' Deeling admitted. 'There's a long list of suspected issues against them from all over. But nothing you can rightly drive a nail in. I can get them for unlawful assault against you and Sam but that's about it.'

'They're bad to the bone though, Sheriff. Better they were kept away from folk.'

'I know it, Jake. But the law is the law.'

Jake sighed. 'Well let me know if they get cut loose, won't you? They may come looking for us again.'

'Of course, I'll give your fair warning. The big one is going even crazier locked up in there. It's like watching a caged cougar as he walks up and down all day long spouting chapter and verse from the Bible. Looks to drive me as crazy as him if I have to listen to it much longer. The other one is getting to walk a piece now, Doc says he'll be dragging one foot along the rest of his days, though.'

'When's the circuit judge due?'

Deeling shrugged. 'He'll be here in about another four weeks. When are you planning to take your remounts up to the fort?'

'Any time now. We're about ready to go, I'm just here in town stocking up for the trip.'

'Well, make sure you're back in time for the trial. I'll need you as witness.'

'We'll be back in good time.' Jake turned to take his leave.

'Er, there's one more thing before you go, Jake.'

There was a quietness to Deeling's voice that warned Jake that it was not good news that was coming. 'This is kind of difficult,' Deeling confessed. 'It's about Sam Parks. Whilst I was looking up the Macafees I came on a reward poster for a bank job some ten years back. It's old news, I know, but the case is still open. Seems a gang of five men hit a bank in New Mexico, one of them was nailed and shot dead during the getaway. They caught two of the other perpetrators and they named all their associates before they were taken out and lynched by the angry townsfolk. One of them named was a certain Sam Parks.'

'Sam!' Jake gasped in surprise. 'I wouldn't put him down as a thief of any kind.'

Deeling shrugged, 'Me neither, but you realize I have to bring him in.'

Jake recognized the sheriff's strict call to duty; he was a man who tried to flavour the letter of the law with intelligence but ultimately he would always answer the call diligently.

'That goes hard, Sheriff. Sam's been a fine hand and he's a good friend now.'

'That's why I'm letting you know this. I don't know the truth of it, after all it's just the word of a couple of outlaws who probably wanted to escape a sad end if they gave up their *compadres*. Still, the question has to be answered. But I'll try to be fair on this, so I have a proposal.' He hesitated a second. 'Ain't exactly legal, you realize, but here's what I aim to do. I'm going to come out to the ranch tomorrow looking to take Sam in. However, if he ain't around, well then I can't do it, can I?'

Jake nodded and a slow grin spread across his face. 'Obliged to you, Sheriff. Could be you'll have a wasted journey.'

Deeling brushed at his moustache and his lean lips spread, echoing Jake's smile. 'I fully expect I will, but just maybe I'll get a fresh cup of coffee out of it.'

They set out early next morning. A yellowish dawn light was cracking through a low lying grey cloud layer that split an otherwise clear sky. The remount herd was spirited and eager to run and they took to the road with little urging. Kitty watched their departure from the porch, holding a lantern high until their dust cloud was out of sight in the gloom.

'Don't you worry none,' assured Clay, who had stayed behind to keep her company. 'Those two know what they're doing.'

Kitty's lip twisted. 'I hope so. I really do. Can't imagine why there was all the rush last night.'

'They're just keen to be going, I guess.'

Neither of them had any idea of the sheriff's impending visit as Jake had chosen not to say anything until he had spoken to Sam. The drive out with the herd precluded any conversation, and although Sam was as surprised as the others at Jake's urgency he said nothing. Yet, as they rode the herd along he cast the occasional glance in Jake's direction, sensing the other's silence indicated some kind of problem.

It was not until mid-morning that the two had an opportunity to have a word. The herd had got over its early morning excitement and had settled to a steady pace, which gave Sam the chance to pull in alongside Jake.

'What's going on, Jake?'

'You feel it, huh?' Jake answered ruefully.

'Sure do. We leave all likety split, with hardly time for a farewell word.'

'I saw the sheriff yesterday,' Jake said, looking into the distance. 'He had something to tell me.'

'That so?' Sam answered quietly.

'Uhuh; seems there's a reward posted for you. Bank job in New Mexico.'

Sam's shoulders sagged. 'So that's it.' He sighed. 'I guess it was bound to catch up to me sometime.'

'He gave you a chance, Sam. Said we had until today to quit the place so he wouldn't have to take you in.'

'Mighty civil of him.'

'He's a decent man alright. You want to talk about it?'

'I made a bad decision, that's all. I had a younger brother back then, he's gone now, God forgive me. He fell in with a bunch of Southern boys who never got over their raiding days from back in the war. I got the word and went to pull him out, I knew it was bound to end badly for him if he stayed with them. He was a good kid, just reckless and a mite stupid. Anyway, the short of it is, I went down there to keep him safe. I never took no money from it, Jake, that's gospel. Didn't want to be involved, just had to keep the boy out of trouble. But I failed miserable even on that score.'

'He was the one killed?'

Sam nodded. 'He was. By then it was too late for me, though; some of the fellows they caught named us all. So I was tarred with the same brush, been ducking it ever since.'

'And the other fellow, the one who got away?'

'Oh, him, he was the leader of the pack. Curly Bright Smith, they call him. He took the cash money saddlebags and made a clean getaway, but not before he put my brother in way of a bullet to save himself. Ten years I been looking for that character. I ever meet up with him it'll be curtains for one or the other of us.'

'So, were you there at the bank?'

'Nope, I was in some cantina feeling sorry for myself and getting stupid drunk. I'd tried to talk the boy out of it but he snuck off and went right on and did the deed without telling me. Thing is the ones they took prisoner wanted easy time, so they drew on as many names as they could to make themselves look good. That's how I got included; alongside my brother's name it made it look like I was in on the whole thing. Folks in that town were pretty riled about losing their savings so there wasn't no point in trying to explain things. Would have meant a long drop on a short rope if I had, just like they did with the others.'

'And you never found this Curly Bright Smith?'

'Nope. Never did.'

'Seems he's the only one can clear you.'

'That's a fact. Kind of unlikely though, knowing his nature.'

'A mean one, huh?'

'As they come. He's up there with the Macafees. One of those who came out of the Civil War learning nothing but killing.'

'Surely though, he'll be an old man now?'

'Not so old, mid-fifties maybe. He started young.'

'Well, I wish you luck with it, Sam. Best you light out once we reach the fort, though. Sheriff Deeling gave you a chance, but he'll have to do the right thing by his reckoning eventually.'

'I know it, Jake. Be sorry to go, though.'

'Be sorry to lose you, partner.'

At about the same hour Younghusband Deeling was making his promised trip out to the Cartright ranch by a different route. He took his time, allowing as much space as he reasonably could for Sam to disappear. He knew in his heart that Sam Parks was no outlaw and reasoned that either plain foolishness or an excess of zeal in his younger days had led him to temporarily take the wrong path. Deeling was of an age where he was becoming a more forgiving type of character; he had seen many wild days on the frontier and watched many men end badly. Little of it had turned out to change things much. If they ever did, he realized, it would be a very long process. And in this frame of mind he was prepared to give someone like Sam Parks the benefit of the doubt.

He was part-way to the ranch, riding under a high hot sun when he saw Christopher Leeward and two of his men, Buck Holdall and Lorn Chaser, waiting on the road ahead.

'Morning, Younghusband,' greeted Leeward. 'This is fortunate, I was just on my way to see you.'

'Gentlemen,' replied Deeling. 'How can I help?'

'It's about the Macafees,' said Leeward. 'We feel you might be being a little too harsh on them.'

'Harsh. How so?'

'Well, they've been locked away for a month now. And one of them wounded bad, too.'

'That was of their own making,' said Deeling. 'They broke the peace and have to wait on a court judgment now.'

'I know it, Sheriff. We fully appreciate your position as law officer but don't you think a little clemency is in order. Might I go their bail for instance, let them stretch their legs awhile?'

Deeling shook his head. 'I don't think so, Mr Leeward. I don't like their style at all. Couple of mad dogs I wouldn't like to see set free amongst the community.'

'Aw, come now,' cut in Buck Holdall. 'Just high-spirited, surely? Way I heard it they was just playing a mite with Rains and Parks. Teasing is all, surely?'

Deeling shook his head. 'Not the way I saw it. Remember, I was there at the time. It's not any hearsay as far as I'm concerned.'

Leeward looked at him long and hard. 'Younghusband, I really would like you to set them loose. Can you do that for me?' There was an obvious undertone of warning in his voice.

'No, sir. I'm elected peace officer for Oakum and I intend to do my duty fully on that score. And I have to say I don't take kindly to any sort of badgering from whatever source. Now I realize you are an important man around these parts, but there's some questions still need answering concerning the theft of the stallion from the Cartright place and how it ended up at the L double E. So, it might be wise if you just give me the road here and let me be on my way.'

Leeward mimicked shock. 'You think I had something to do with that, Sheriff? Why, I declare! How could you think such a thing?'

'Isn't hard, Mr Leeward, when the stolen property ends up on your ranch.'

Leeward frowned. 'I believe I take deep offence at that, Younghusband. I really do. I don't think I can let such a thing pass unanswered.'

Deeling heard the sound of hoofbeats behind him as a horse left the roadside bushes and pulled up to his rear, it was followed by the ominous snick of a rifle being cocked.

'A bad move, Leeward,' warned Deeling, knowing with certainty that his moment had come. He brushed aside his coat tail to reach his pistol in what he already knew was a vain attempt to make a stand.

'Bad for you, Younghusband,' drawled Leeward with a smile.

'Let him have it, Cole.'

Reichter fired the Winchester rapidly from a few feet behind and the sheriff tumbled forward, his horse bucking wildly at the shots and throwing the limp body to lie crumpled on the dusty road.

CHAPTER NINE

Fort Brill had been an old log fort in the frontier days but since then it had been expanded and now stretched into a large 800-by 500-foot quadrangle with two watchtowers and a ten foot high stockade wall. There were four companies on station there and the walls housed a hospital, library, bakery and barracks as well as storehouses, magazine and guardhouse.

Jake had ridden on ahead and had a corral prepared for their herd of remounts outside the fort walls. Once the herd was driven in and checked over, the two men were led by a hostelry sergeant across the parade ground to meet the commanding officer.

'Best guard your step,' warned the sergeant, a grizzled and bearded veteran of Irish origin. 'The dear colonel has himself a newfangled toy.'

As they rounded the corner to the administrative building a loud bang made all three duck instinctively. They were met by the sudden appearance of a strange four-wheeled beast in red and gold which weaved towards them at a lumbering pace. Sitting atop steering the creature was the colonel, a broad grin of excitement creasing his face.

'What the hell is that?' asked Jake fearfully, as the thing clattered and puttered nearer.

'That there is the future,' said the sergeant ruefully. 'A mechanical working carriage. Runs on nothing but gasoline, would you believe?'

'Well I never,' gasped Sam. 'You mean it runs along on its own like a steam-train without rails?'

'Sure does.'

The vehicle pulled to a squeaking and steamy halt and the colonel, an energetic, red-faced chubby man looked down at them from his leather seat.

'What's this, Sergeant Coster?'

The sergeant drew himself up and saluted. 'These here men brought in the remounts I told you about, sir. Need to draw their fee from the quartermaster on your say-so.'

'Well, gentlemen,' said the colonel, introducing himself as he got down from his steed. 'Pleased to meet you, Colonel Moodie at your service.' The three shook hands and Colonel Moodie turned to the sergeant again. 'You happy with the mounts, Sergeant?'

'Yes sir, they look fine and all broke ready to ride.'

'Excellent. Well then, you have a bill of sale, gentlemen?'

Jake passed him the ready-made document.

'Then we'll get this signed off for you right away.'

'Colonel,' said Sam, indicating the vehicle. 'Forgive me asking but what is that wagon thing you have there?'

'That, sir,' said the colonel proudly, 'is the Winton Phaeton horseless carriage. Cost me a pretty penny I can tell you; had her imported special from the works in Cleveland. Worth one thousand dollars in all.'

Jake blew a whistle, 'Sure is a fine-looking thing, but what do you use it for?'

'Why, transport of course. She'll run for some twenty-five miles on a gallon of gasoline at a constant speed of fifty miles an hour. There's an equivalent of six horsepower in there.' He chuckled smugly. 'And with gasoline at seven cents a gallon I fear she'll be doing you horse traders out of business some day soon.'

Jake wrinkled his nose. 'Can't see that, Colonel. At a thousand dollars a hit it'll be a mite more expensive than a four-legged pony to my way of thinking.'

'Mark my words, Mr Rains. This'll be the way of it in days to come. I foresee the time when all the US military will be running around in these vehicles.'

Jake looked doubtful but politely declined to argue with the officer as they followed him into his office.

They decided on a meal at the sutler's store once they had been paid off. Their mood was jovial with the poke of money safely tucked in their saddlebags and they ordered a celebratory bottle to share as they seated themselves at a table in the busy store.

Off duty servicemen and a few civilians crowded the place, some favouring the long bartop service counter whilst other smoked a pipe or cheroot over a glass or two seated at the tables populating the body of the store.

The sutler's burly aproned wife came over and took their order; whilst they waited they cracked open the bottle and savoured the liquor.

'You think that horseless carriage'll ever catch on?' Sam asked over his glass.

'Can't see it myself,' Jake answered. 'Can you imagine that thing heading down a rock canyon or fording a full riverbed? Hell, you'd hear it coming a mile away as well, with all that clatter; damned sure it'd frighten the life out of any livestock.'

'Stinks something awful too,' agreed Sam.

The sutler's wife returned with a basket of bread and two large oval plates covered with giant steaks and a mess of fried potatoes and boiled greens. 'Looks good,' said Jake with a grin as he dug in. 'I can sure do with this.'

They had barely started when Jake was startled as Sam suddenly dropped his cutlery onto his plate with a loud clatter. He looked up to see Sam staring white-faced over his shoulder at the bar behind.

'What?' asked Jake, twisting to see behind. 'What's up, Sam?'

'He's here,' whispered Sam hoarsely.

Jake ran his eyes over the men standing at the bar, 'Who?

91

What're you talking about?'

'There on the end. The one with the bearskin and the round-top hat, you see him?'

Jake picked out the man, a burly fellow with a bearskin coat over a black suit jacket and pants. He wore a close-fitting bowler hat and was munching on a fair-sized meat sandwich. A quiet, solemn-looking fellow with a glazed distant stare that ignored the bustle around him.

'Curly Bright Smith,' whispered Sam. 'As sure as I'm sitting here.'

'You reckon?' asked Jake doubtfully.

'I do.' So saying, Sam pushed back his chair and rose, unfastening the leather loop on his Colt's hammer as he did so.

'Steady, Sam,' warned Jake. 'This here is Government property, they won't take kindly to any trouble.'

Ignoring him, Sam called across the room. 'Curly Bright Smith!' he shouted loudly.

The room quieted instantly, all eyes turning towards Sam. Only a sea of tobacco smoke stood between Sam and the man at the bar, who froze with the sandwich half in his mouth. The man chewed a moment, then laid aside the sandwich.

'You talking to me?' he asked.

'You remember a lad, name of Parks down in New Mexico?' asked Sam.

The man swallowed, and licked a crumb of bread from his lip. 'I do,' he admitted with a slow nod.

'You remember how he took a bullet for you?'

There was a scrabble of feet at that as customers ducked to one side out of the line of fire.

'I do,' admitted the man again.

'You remember how you put him in way of that bullet?'

'To my shame, brother, I do.'

'I ain't your brother but that boy was mine and now I aim to call you out on that score, Curly Bright.'

Curly Bright slowly pulled aside his bearskin coat to show he was unarmed, he also tugged aside a loose neckerchief at his throat to expose a white preacher's collar.

'Do as you will,' he said. 'I have it coming, it is true. It was a sin I live with all my days.'

Sam crouched tensely, his fingers hooked ready over the handle of his pistol. 'Get yourself a gun, Curly Bright,' he hissed; then, more loudly. 'Someone give him a pistol.'

A watching cavalryman unbuttoned his service Colt from its holster.

'Here you go, fella. I want to see how this pans out.' He grinned at his fellow soldiers as he spun the weapon down the length of the bar-top.

'No more,' said Curly Bright, ignoring the pistol. 'I saw the light five years back and swore off it. You're Sam Parks, yes?'

Sam nodded.

'Forgive me then,' Curly Bright went on. 'I did you and your family grave wrong. True to say, in them days I was all devil-led and mean as a rattler, I know it. But like Saint Paul it come to me in a blinding vision to give up them days of wickedness and to follow a more righteous path.'

'I don't believe you,' snarled Sam.

Curly Bright shrugged calmly. 'I follow the way of the Lord now, Brother Parks. If you must take my life for a payback then you have every right. I was a no account vicious sinner and it is my due, of that there can be no doubt.'

Sam faltered at the man's calm confession. 'You mean to just stand there and let me gun you down?' he asked.

'I do,' said Curly Bright, opening his arms wide and closing his eyes. 'Do your worst, Brother Parks. I am ready. Before God in heaven, I am ready.'

Sam straightened, a confused look spreading across his face. Slowly his hand withdrew from the pistol grip. 'Dammit, man. You leave me little choice, if you won't fight me.'

Curly Bright opened his eyes. 'I swear to you, Brother Parks, I have left those ways behind me. I travel now, spreading words of peace and love instead of greed and violence. The Lord Jesus has entered my heart and there is no room in there for licentiousness and war.'

'It's true,' a voice called from the back of the room. 'He holds service here each week come Sunday.'

Agreement followed from different sources. 'That's right, he leads a congregation here.'

Jake moved back his chair and stood placing a restraining hand on Sam's arm. 'Well then, Preacher Smith, as it seems, why don't you come on over here and join us? Have a word with my friend Sam here and settle this matter.'

'Surely, I will.'

Sam backed off a pace as Curly Bright crossed the room, weaving between tables as he came to them. 'Don't trust him, Jake,' Sam warned. 'He's devious as a sidewinder.'

Curly Bright drew up a chair and sat, spreading his hands, the fingers flat on the tabletop. He looked up at Sam with a slightly questioning frown crossing his brow.

Jake sat down whilst Sam still stood aside, tense and ready. A low mumble of conversation returned to the room as if collectively the crowd instinctively knew there was to be no gunplay.

Sam drew his pistol and laid it on the table before him as he sat down, glaring steadily at Curly Bright all the while.

Curly Bright nodded. 'Truly,' he said 'I am at your command. Whatever I can do in restitution.'

'Well,' said Jake thoughtfully. 'You could give Sam here written evidence that he played no part in that robbery. Give him a clean sheet against the wanted bill that's out on him.'

Again Curly Bill nodded. 'I will. Before witnesses I will do it.'

Sam was not so easily satisfied. 'You took my brother's life. Pressed him before you to take a killing shot to the heart whilst you ran off with the cash money.'

Curly Bill hung his head. 'I did,' he admitted. 'Even now the thought fills me with remorse. You must see, Brother Parks, that I am cursed by my past. Tortured by the things I did and have to

94

make good. My days are spent in that task, it is the only way I can go on living.'

'More than my brother can,' spat Sam. 'He was just a kid, man. A young boy with little sense in his head and too much life in his body.'

'You think he was the only one?' Curly Bill looked up, an angry flash momentarily lighting his eyes. 'I killed many, Brother Parks. Men good and bad, innocent women and children, Indians, dogs, cats anything that crossed my path when the drink was upon me. I live with their ghosts. I would it was not this way. Why the Good Lord came to me and cursed me so is a mystery I have no way of understanding. But he did and here I am, ravaged by it all.'

Sam turned to Jake. 'You believe this?' he asked, his face twisted in disgust.

Jake nodded slowly. 'I think I do,' he said.

Sam paused, taking a long moment to consider it. 'Then write it out and at least get the law off my back,' he said with mordant bitterness.

Curly Bright looked at Sam sadly. 'Thank you, Brother Parks. We shall do it before officers here. Doubtless it will mean my being charged with the crime but that will be a punishment I accept gladly if it eases your soul and mine.'

And so it was done. Inevitably Curly Bright was taken into custody whilst his admissions were investigated and Jake and Sam were allowed to go their way, a copy of the confession safely tucked in Sam's saddlebag. Before they left, though, the colonel made them a surprising offer. He advised them to go before the Governor and the judiciary at the state capital in Lincoln with himself as guarantor and in that manner they could be sure that the wanted postings in Sam's name were withdrawn more speedily. The two men were doubtful, as the expedition would mean many days away from the ranch where Kitty and Clay were managing on their own. But the colonel obviously saw an opportunity to experiment with his new vehicle and offered to take them there in the machine. He promised that they could make the trip in two days in the horseless carriage and be back at the fort within seven.

It was a tempting offer and, although a shade reluctant, Jake and Sam agreed.

The colonel had his adjutant arrange everything for their departure and it was with some trepidation that Jake and Sam mounted the strange-looking vehicle. It was primarily a two-seater, so the padded seat up front was a trifle cramped with the three of them squeezed in, but Colonel Moodie ignored the discomfort; he was in jovial mood and obviously excited about the whole venture.

'See here, boys. These knobs and levers here change the gears and I steer by the tiller. Have to admit I'm not quite competent at the steering yet awhile, but we'll get her right as we go along.' He turned to his captain who was waiting in attendance below them. 'You have the cans of gasoline loaded, Captain?'

'I do, sir. All's ready, they're lashed on behind. Have a safe passage.'

'Thank you, Captain. I leave the fort in your capable hands. We'll be back in a week's time.'

'God and the Fates willing,' muttered Sam dubiously.

Just before leaving the colonel had the leather bonnet raised against the heat of the sun and they set off with a chundering splutter through the fort gates. Lines of curious troops marked their departure and the waiting men raised a ragged cheer and offered a few ribald comments as they left. The colonel led a veering path out as he accustomed himself with the steering bar, narrowly missing the gateposts as he went. Jake bit his lip as the vehicle's rubber wheels zigzagged from one side of the rutted wagon road to the other. Luckily it was a well used route and flat and wide in most places, which enabled the colonel's initial learning drive to be made without too much danger to other traffic on the road. Jake was suddenly surprised to find he had caught hold and was holding on to Sam's arm with a fearful steely grip, and he gave Sam an apologetic nod as he released him. The two cowboys stared nervously ahead without saying a word as the colonel changed up into second gear and sped on.

Free of the fort, they passed herds of grazing cattle and bemused reservation Indians standing at the roadside. With a chuckle, the colonel squeezed his rubber-valved horn. At the honking sound the cattle ran off in terror and the Indians dived to the ground to take cover. The colonel laughed uproariously, obviously enjoying himself hugely, whilst Jake and Sam stared white-faced at the void before them where normally a team of horses would be racing ahead. It was all a new and terrifying experience for the two cowboys.

CHAPTER TEN

In Oakum meanwhile, Leeward was busily reinforcing his plans for complete control over the town. He collected his three henchmen together in the town office and set out his plan.

'First off,' he said to the trio who lounged before him. 'We need to do this legal. At least apparently so. We want no repercussions from outside at State level, you understand?'

They did not but they nodded all the same. They were men who had done much as they wished all their lives without any forethought or care for the results of their actions, and the concept of a distant outside influence was beyond their consideration. But Leeward knew that in these modern times, if any telegraphed whisper reached the State legislature of irregular activities, even in this backwater township, the powers that be would be forced into sending someone from the marshal's office to investigate.

Leeward went on with mocking solemnity, 'We have no peace officer here now, due to the sad demise of poor Younghusband Deeling.'

The three gunslingers sniggered dutifully.

'I think,' Leeward went on, 'it is only fitting that you, Cole, should fill his boots. What do you say?'

Reichter smiled. 'Sure thing. I'd like that. Running things around here would suit me fine.'

'No, Cole,' snapped Leeward quickly. 'You don't run things around here, I do. Don't you forget it. Now, pay close attention.

When we have you in office you will release the Macafees, on lack of evidence or some such excuse. They'll go their way and we'll let them get on with what they started out to do and finish off Rains and his friends. You got that?'

Reichter nodded dutifully.

'I shall run for the office of town mayor,' Leeward went on. 'Then when I have the town safely in my hands we make move on the Cartright place. I'll get my bank to foreclose on the property and buy it up for a song. You boys will all get a piece of that; it will be yours to divide up as you will. Least I can do for all your loyalty. How's that grab you fellows?'

'Why, that's mighty generous of you, Mr Leeward.' Buck Holdall uttered his thanks with a surprised grin. 'Think on it, boys. We'll have our own place all to ourselves. Do as we want, when we want.'

'Why not?' said Leeward. 'I'll have more than enough, why shouldn't you have some too? Without you boys none of this would be possible.' With this promise of largesse Leeward bound them to him, and he could see by the gleam in their eyes that he had judged correctly and now had their confirmed loyalty.

'How're you going to get me to be sheriff though, Mr Leeward?' asked Reichter doubtfully. 'They ain't gonna vote for me.'

'Of course they will, Cole. We'll have elections and without any other candidates in evidence you'll romp home.'

'No other candidates. How's that?'

'We'll just have to make sure there ain't any,' supplied Buck Holdall knowingly.

Reichter thought about it, then a smile grew as the notion slowly sunk in. 'Oh, yeah. I get it. Yeah, I like that. No candidates but me, huh?'

Leeward raised his eyes skywards in despair, 'Yes, that's it, Cole. You get to be sheriff and I get to be mayor. We'll have this town sewn up so tight that nothing will happen without our say-so.'

'It's OK, Mr Leeward,' yukked Reichter. 'You'll be mayor

alright. We'll just make sure there's no other candidates in evidence, right?'

'Now you're getting the picture, Cole, you dumb ass,' laughed Buck Holdall.

'One thing though,' warned Leeward sternly, cutting off their jollity. 'Nothing befalls Kitty Cartright. I have plans for that pretty, stuck-up miss. She is mine and before I am done with her she will be eating her pride and following me around like a dog on a lead.'

'Yeah, we understand,' said Buck Holdall slyly. He knew of Kitty's rejection and saw in Leeward's reaction a crack of weakness he knew he could use to his advantage if it ever came to it. 'She's all yours, Mr Leeward. Didn't think for one moment she'd come to us along with the ranch as well.'

'So, to work. I want handbills printed advising of elections for mayor and sheriff. And you boys will post them all over the town. Set it up for three days hence, we don't want to waste any time.'

Oakum entered into a time of subtle intimidation and Leeward's earlier generous ways stood him in good stead as the townsfolk overlooked the pressure applied to them and took his smiling advice at face value. It was with a willing acceptance that he was made mayor. Cole Reichter's rise to town sheriff was not so readily accepted, but any competition in the election was intimidated into standing down, so by virtue of there being no other applicants, he finally got the job.

With a new bravado filling him, Reichter entered the jailhouse on his first day in office and spent a casual half-hour exploring the dusty desk drawers and trying out the round-backed chair that had been empty since Deeling's demise.

'Yessir, I like this alright,' he said to himself contentedly as he discovered a half empty whiskey bottle and toasted himself liberally with it. With a grin he fastened the tin star to his vest and polished it with his sleeve. 'Sheriff Cole Reichter', he said aloud to himself, pleased with the sound of it.

He heard the mutterings coming from the cell out back and

remembered Leeward's instructions. He took the heavy key from the drawer and made his way back there.

'Morning, boys,' he said cheerfully. 'New day here in Oakum.'

'What's this?' asked Ezekiel from his bunk.

'I'm the newly elected town sheriff for Oakum right now,' supplied Reichter, turning the key in the lock. 'And my first task in office is to set you fellows free.'

Abraham glowered at him suspiciously. 'How come?' he grunted.

'Well,' Reichter shrugged, 'there's no case against you as far as I'm concerned.'

'Where's Deeling?' asked Ezekiel.

'Oh, Sheriff Deeling was found on the road out of town. He won't be around no more. Poor fellow was shot down by parties unknown. I'll have to investigate that little matter soon as I feel the inclination.' Reichter grinned at them in a confidential way.

Abraham pushed open the cell door and drew a deeply suspicious breath. 'This wouldn't be some type of deceit, now would it, Brother Reichter? We don't go down and meet our end as escaping prisoners or some such, do we?'

'No, no,' assured Reichter. 'You're free as air. Your long guns are out there in the office. Take them and go where you will.'

Abraham made his way to the office to see the truth of it. Ezekiel pulled himself awkwardly to his feet and limped after his brother, dragging his ruined leg as he went. The two backwoodsmen took their rifles down from the rack and immediately began to check the action.

'What's brought this on?' asked Abraham.

'Like I say, new order here in town now. Mr Leeward is the town mayor and I'm peace officer. We run things here now, so what we say goes.'

'Right comfortable for you,' observed Ezekiel.

'Something you might like to know, though. . . .' Reichter hesitated.

'Speak,' said Abraham solemnly.

'Them two cowboys. Jake Rains and Sam Parks, they made their way up to Fort Brill with their herd of remounts. Should be heading back any time now.'

'So,' chuckled Ezekiel, dragging his fingers through his unkempt beard. 'That's it. We get set free to go finish those two thorns in Leeward's side.'

'Makes no matter the cause, Brother,' said Abraham. 'We need to make those two pay for the killings they made against us. I need to rain fire and brimstone on the heads of them unrighteous.'

'Indeed, Brother Abe,' agreed Ezekiel. 'But let us first taste some strong liquor. It's been a long while without such refreshment.'

Abraham harrumphed a grunt of acceptance and the two brushed past Reichter and out of the jailhouse, carrying their rifles as they went.

Later that same day, Leeward, Buck Holdall and Lorn Chaser were holding court in Leeward's town office when Clay Rudebaugh turned up. He had come into Oakum to see Leeward about the wages he was owed and, although a little nervous about the prospect, it was still a mission he felt duty bound to fulfil as Kitty was running short of cash. After all, he considered it was his due for the time he had spent working on Leeward's ranch.

'Lookee here,' cried Buck Chaser as Clay entered. 'If it ain't old Clay, our long-departed cowhand. How you been, Clay?'

'Fair to middling, thank you.'

Leeward pushed back his chair and smiled benignly. 'Good to see you, Mr Rudebaugh. I hear you've been working over at the Cartright place. Glad to see such a neighbourly attitude. I hope Mrs Cartright is well; she hasn't been around town much lately.'

'It's well enough out there, Mr Leeward.'

'So, Clay. How can we help you? Decided to come back and join us at the L double E? After all, the way I hear it, they don't pay much at the Cartright's.'

'No, that ain't it, Mr Leeward. I come here to get what I'm owed. I got three months' wages coming, I guess.'

Leeward raised his eyebrows. 'Three months? Is that so. Well now, I don't know about that.'

Clay wrinkled his lip. 'That's the time, Mr Leeward. I recollect it well enough. Three months in all, give or take a day or so.'

'Now, now, Clay,' said Buck Holdall with an easy grin. 'You can't be claiming on that. Why you walked off without a word. Not a single word. Just upped and went off to work elsewhere with no notice whatsoever. Now, that ain't proper and right, to my way of thinking.'

'Be that as it may,' said Clay firmly. 'I'm still owed for my time.'

Buck Holdall gnawed on a matchstick held between his teeth, 'So you just do what you want when you want to, that it Clay? How about us, though? We're suddenly a man short. Now it'd be a fine thing if every working hand behaved like you and just walked off when they felt like it. Leave us in a right pretty pickle, wouldn't it?'

'I didn't come here to argue the point,' said Clay. 'I quit is all and now I'm asking for what's coming to me for my time.'

At that Leeward's face slowly changed, the pleasantness slipping away to be replaced with a cold hard stare. 'Fair enough,' he said. 'You want paying? Well, I'll tell you what, I'll give you what I think you're worth.' With that, he dug into his vest pocket and brought out a single silver dollar coin. Flicking with his thumb, he spun it across the desk to fall with a rattle at Clay's feet. 'There you go,' he said coldly. 'Now take your wages and get out.'

Clay looked down in dismay. 'That ain't enough, Mr Leeward. I got more than that coming my way.'

'Sure you do,' said Lorn Chaser, sliding from the shadowy corner he occupied. 'You got interest coming your way.'

With that he drew his pistol and cocking back the hammer

103

held the barrel pressed to Clay's chest. 'You must want some lead to go with that silver, cowboy?' The gunslinger leered at Clay menacingly.

'Hey now,' said Clay backing off, his hands held wide. 'There's no need for that, I just come asking for my dues.'

'And that's just what you're going to get,' said Buck Holdall, drawing his own revolver and moving in from Clay's other side. 'We don't like traitors at the L double E. Seems to me a little pistol-whipping is in order here. Wouldn't want any old cowhand thinking he can just get up and go over to help out Jake Rains now, would we?'

'Outside with it, boys. Take him round back,' ordered Leeward, with a slow smile. 'You going to make example of this fellow, we can't have it in the mayor's office. That would be most unseemly.'

Obediently, the two closed in on Clay and forced him back through the rear storage room and out into the alleyway beyond.

CHAPTER ELEVEN

The journey to the capital had proved to be more difficult than the colonel had first estimated. The road had been washed away by storms in places, making it necessary to carry the carriage around the debris. Stout poles were placed through the spokes of the wheels and the whole vehicle was lifted by the men, who manhandled it over the obstructions. Then there was a river to ford, which needed the making of a flatbed raft to carry the Phaeton. None of this would have been necessary if they had been on horseback, Jake considered. But once across and on a downhill slope, the speed was incredible and when they'd become acclimatized to the vehicle both Jake and Sam enjoyed the pell mell ride down, whooping and hollering like children on a snow sled.

News of their journey had reached the capital before them, thanks to telegraph messages sent from Fort Brill, and they were greeted with a carnival atmosphere of cheering crowds and much acclaim, being the first of such vehicles to make such a long cross-country journey. The colonel was praised by his peers in the military and Brigadier Billy Starking Crook, who was in town on an inspection tour, took the colonel under his wing and requested a full report of the trip and on the viability of horseless carriages that he might take to show the War Department in Washington.

The Governor, on hearing of the strange carriage's arrival, also lauded the colonel as captain of the daring expedition. Jake and Sam were somewhat marginalized by the hoo-hah and it took some days before the colonel remembered them and arranged an interview with the Governor.

Once that was concluded, their business settled and Sam now reconstituted as an innocent man, they were wined and dined by various officials and businessmen who wished to hear all about the machine and its capabilities. It was at one such meeting that the bet was made.

'So,' said Brigadier Billy, from the table head. 'Colonel Moodie, in your reckoning this machine of yours could outride any horse?'

They were seated in the Cattlemen's Association dining rooms, a lavishly furnished hall with oak-panelled walls decorated with framed portraits of past officials and mounted examples of wide-winged longhorns that had once adorned prize bulls.

'Why, of course, sir,' said the colonel, flushed with confidence and a little too much wine. 'Think on it. There's no need to feed the beast except for the odd drink of gasoline, and at its top speed my Phaeton will outrun any mount for longer and further. It is a machine, sir. It does not think, nor does it argue. It cannot fall ill or drop dead, it will just go on and on.' The colonel made this wildly outrageous and inaccurate statement with all the firm assurance that only praise and alcohol will engender.

'And what about you, Mr Rains?' said the brigadier, turning to Jake. 'How say you? I dare say you are a horseman of merit, being one of the Rough Riders. What's your opinion?'

'Well, sir,' answered Jake, 'there's no doubting its speed. That old cart can lay down a fair lick, and that's the truth. But for transport over rough country, I doubt she'll be up to the task.'

'So, you would say that there is no future for the military in such vehicles?'

'I doubt it, sir. A pony can climb a mountain, slide down a gully. Swim a river and handle all kinds of terrain. Can't say that about a horseless carriage. She's just fine as long as the land is flat without obstruction, but beyond that I don't know as she'd do so well.'

'Tosh!' said the colonel, a little irritated. 'Come on, Jake. You saw how she went and we managed just fine.'

Jake declined to argue and just shook his head doubtfully.

'Well, sirs,' said the brigadier. 'How about a little trial of sorts? Would be a fine help for your country in proving the worth of the mechanical against horseflesh. Colonel, you and these men are bound to take the same road back to Fort Brill, are you not? Why not try a little race. We have two fine horsemen here, let them ride out and, Colonel, you take your machine and the first to reach the fort wins the day and proves the veracity of his words.'

The cattlemen at the table boisterously pounded their fists at this and called out agreement at the challenge. Already the sound of shouting voices calling out side bets was heard. Jake looked across at Sam, his eyes wide with question and Sam gave him a slight shrug and a smile in return.

'I'll do it,' bawled Colonel Moodie merrily. 'What do you good fellows say?' he asked.

'Sure thing, Colonel. What the hell, we'll give it a go,' agreed Jake. 'Long as we get to pick the mounts.'

'Done then,' said Brigadier Billy. 'You can have the pick of the cavalry stables here and you, Colonel Moodie, will have two servicemen to accompany you to equal your weight on the trip out. How does that sound?'

'Fair enough indeed, sir.' The colonel grinned amenably, reaching across the table to shake Jake and Sam by the hand.

CHAPTER TWELVE

The Macafees drank themselves to a standstill. Whereas they saw sin in practically every area of daily life they saw none in an over-abundance of grain liquor. They finished off their first night of freedom in a stupor on the board floor of the Barrel of Beer. No one thought to argue with them or interrupt their orgy of indul-gence and any of the few customers who were remaining there in the early hours merely stepped over their supine bodies and made their various ways home without a backward glance.

The two brothers awakened in the same grim mood as was their normal state of mind, and after struggling to digest a full breakfast with the help of a few draughts of beer they set out to find themselves mounts. Leeward had foreseen this requirement and had Cole Reichter supply them with two saddled and sup-plied beasts ready for the road. It was in Leeward's mind that the sooner the troublesome pair were on their way the better it would be for him and for what he now considered to be his town.

The two received the donated mounts without a word of thanks and went off looking for their brother's grave to pay their last respects. They found the town cemetery on the way north out of Oakum and searched the painted wooden markers until they discovered Absalom's resting-place. Here, Abraham fell solidly to his knees and, bowing his head, clasped his hands together in prayer, whilst Ezekiel, favouring his wounded leg, stood near by, holding the horses.

'Dearest brother,' mumbled Abraham to the mounded earth

before him. 'I weep to see ye laid out under this sod. But we know you have gone on to a better place. We are promised there is milk and honey aplenty there. Cleave to your brother Mose who has gone on before. Rest easy. I swear that Ezekiel and I shall seek out those that harmed ye, they shall sleep at your feet before long, I promise thou this. The Devil shall take their black souls for all their wickedness and they shall burn eternally in that demon's pit, but only after we have exacted our own justice upon them. Amen, brother. Amen, I say to that.'

Abraham raised himself from his knees and stood for a moment staring down at the pale marker, a solitary tear rolling down his hairy cheek. He turned sharply and gave a nod to Ezekiel, and the two mounted up and rode off.

They rode north, following the supply road that led to Fort Brill.

The brothers kept their eyes peeled, expecting to see a returning Jake and Sam at every turn of the road, but it was not until they reached the fort itself that they learned of the events that had delayed the two cowboys' return. A verbose sutler told them the whole tale, from the finding of Curly Bright Smith to the vehicle ride to the capital and the expected race back. The whole fort had received news of the race by telegraph and this in turn had raised an excited fever of gambling throughout the fort's occupants, for which the sutler himself kept the book.

Abraham and Ezekiel received the news with an apparent lack of concern and seated themselves at a vacant table to decide on their next step.

'This Preacher Smith is of interest to me,' confided Abraham. 'A man who has received The Word. A man of righteous spirit and calling and yet one who in the past has smote down those who opposed him.'

'Indeed, Brother,' agreed Ezekiel vaguely. His leg aggravated him and gave him constant pain which did nothing to ease his already dark mood. He rubbed aggressively at the offending limb as if that would relieve the ache.

'Could he be of use to us, d'ye think?' asked Abraham.

'In what way?'

'He knows this Parks. Must know him well from his sinful days. Might be he could assist us in bringing Parks into our hands.'

'We work best alone, Brother Abe. It has always been that way. Outsiders never understand the fashion of our means.'

'Ye speak truth, Ezekiel. Remember though, now we are only two. It could be we must think anew.'

'How so?'

'There are many that shall travel to that iniquitous city I should liken to Gomorrah. Ye have heard them speak of this race they are about. Many will line the pathway, will come to watch and be abroad. It will not be so easy, I think.'

'Then what? We take the preacher from his prison cell here. What if he will not come and if he does come will not favour us with assistance?'

Abraham pulled at his lower lip thoughtfully, scratching into his beard as he did so. He leant forward, his voice low in cunning, 'He will be a shield to us, whatever he chooses. Parks has complaint against him for slaying his sibling. In that fashion we may use this preacher by way of diversion.'

Ezekiel nodded. 'I see value in that. More so than as one who will turn his hand to our side. It could be that as the staked lamb leads the wolf to the trap, then in the same way this preacher might lure Parks into ours.'

'Well said, Ezekiel.'

'It is a risk, Brother.'

'I know it, but my blood is up. I am stirred with zeal. My right hand is full of thunderbolts and my left holds the whirlwind. The spirit is on me like a heavenly fire.' Abraham's voice began to rise as his passion increased. 'Mine eyes see only swords of fire descending. . . .'

Ezekiel laid a staying hand on Abraham's wrist as he noticed other customers beginning to take an interest in them.

110

'Be still, Abe. Calm yourself, let not the fever take your senses.'

Breathing hard through his nostrils, Abraham sought to control the madness that rose in his chest. He clenched his jaw and his eyes rolled up in his skull. 'I must have their heads, Ezekiel,' he hissed, forcing himself to remain still in his seat even though his body twitched with the desire for vengeance.

'It shall be so,' Ezekiel soothed. 'Let us go then, and see how we might take this preacher to ourselves.'

The guardhouse, they discovered, was set next to the officers' barracks. It had a solitary guard outside. Normally there would be no guards, but as the prisoner was of a sensitive civilian category it had been decided to place a mobile sentry outside.

The two backwoodsmen saw soldiers move in and out of the guardhouse as they watched during the afternoon and estimated that a permanent staff of two were usually stationed inside the jail. Their curiosity satisfied, they withdrew again to the sutler's store to await the descent of nightfall.

When the shadows were fallen, they made their way to the stables and prepared their horses for a quick getaway. A third mount was added surreptitiously, a cavalry mount, to carry their prospective fugitive.

Then, forest-trained as they were to use the darkness, they slid silently around the side wall of the guardhouse. As the injury to Ezekiel's leg now made it impossible for him to move swiftly, he was to act as a diversion.

The bored guard leant against the jailhouse wall, dumbly staring off into space as he waited impatiently for his relief.

'Ho, soldier!' said Ezekiel, approaching him openly.

'Hold up,' said the soldier, raising his rifle. 'No civilians allowed here.'

'But there is something amiss,' warned Ezekiel, nodding vaguely in the direction of the shadowed alley between the jailhouse and officers' barracks.

'What's that?' asked the guard, looking over his shoulder.

'Some masked men, sneaking there in the shadows. I think they're up to no good.'

'You seen 'em?'

'Here, look.' Ezekiel beckoned. 'They made their way down here. They were carrying ropes and barrels. It seemed a bit strange to me.'

The guard's curiosity got the better of him and he followed Ezekiel close to the alley mouth. With a quick glance up at the parapet guards, Ezekiel nodded an all-clear to Abraham and there was a dull thud as the guard was brought to his knees by Abraham's rifle butt. A second blow and the man was prostrate, the two brothers quickly pulling the unconscious guard out of sight into the shadows. Ezekiel bent down, picked up the man's forage cap and placed it cockily on his head.

Without a word the two quickly moved to the guardhouse doorway. The guard sergeant inside opened the sliding peephole at their knock and the saw the silhouetted outline of a bearded soldier with his uniform cap perched awkwardly on his head.

'What's up?' asked the sergeant.

'Prisoner requested a Bible, I've brought it over from the chaplain.'

'That a fact?' grumbled the sergeant, taking the key from his belt and unlocking the door. 'You'd best give it here then. And when you get back you get your hair cut, soldier. You look like a damned walking bush out there. . . .' He froze as the Sharps prodded him in the stomach.

'Not a word,' warned Ezekiel grimly. 'And all will be well with thee.'

The sergeant slowly raised his hands and backed away. His assistant, looking up from the dime novel he was reading at sound of the door opening, half rose from his seat as he saw the sergeant's hands reaching skywards.

'Stay!' snapped Abraham, slipping in behind Ezekiel and covering the soldier.

The two soldiers stood with their hands raised as the brothers looked around the guardhouse.

'Where be the preacher, the one they call Curly Bright Smith?' asked Abraham.

'He's through there,' said the sergeant, nodding his head towards an adjoining door that led to the cells. 'But think on it, fellas. You don't want to do this. Have a heap of trouble fall on your heads you set him loose.'

'Have a heap fall on yourn you don't keep quiet,' warned Ezekiel. 'Where's the keys?'

The sergeant dropped his chin to indicate the loop at his belt and Ezekiel snatched them from him.

'Now, lead the way,' he ordered the two soldiers.

The line of windowless prison cages were unoccupied except for the one that held Curly Bright, who was quietly sitting on the edge of his bunk and looked up questioningly as the four men entered. Curly Bright had now entered into a slightly dazed condition, his guilt and constant prayers driving him into a confused state of excessive penitence. He fully expected the ultimate penalty for his crimes and had unconsciously prepared by dissociating himself from what was going on around him. In such a state the appearance of the men in the cells was all a part of a vague dream to him.

'What's going on, Sergeant? Is it time for trial?' he asked.

'Your buddies here come to get you out, I guess,' answered the sergeant.

Curly Bright looked at the two grimly hirsute and buckskin-clad men. 'Who are you two and what do you want with me?' he asked.

'Why, we've come to take ye safely off,' said Ezekiel, unlocking his cage door. 'Ye be a friend of Sam Parks, be ye not?'

'Sam Parks sent you?' replied a confused Curly Bright.

'Not 'xactly,' supplied Ezekiel. 'Just get on out here and come along with us.'

'Not sure that I want to do that.' Curly Bright frowned doubtfully.

Impetuously, Abraham lunged forward, grasped both jacket lapels in his fist and jerked the prisoner out of the cell. 'Ye'll come with us, like it or not.'

Ezekiel ushered the two guards into the cell with the barrel of his rifle. 'Stay there and be still. No good hollering, no one will hear ye through them walls and someone will come by in good time to set ye free. Spend your time to your best avail in prayer and think on the benefits of a good Christian life.' With that he slammed the cell door shut and locked it.

Complaining, Curly Bright was hustled from the guardhouse and into the shadows outside. 'What are you fellows doing?' he cried. 'Are you executioners come to take my life? Does Sam Parks want me dead now?'

'Shut thy mouth,' hissed Abraham, cuffing Curly Bright about the head. 'Or thee will meet thy Maker sooner than ye think.'

'We shall take thee free without harm being done to thee,' reassured Ezekiel more gently. 'Be still, Preacher. Hold thy tongue lest the soldiers take heed. Now come along with confidence. All is well.'

'But no, brothers,' begged Curly Bright. 'I am a sinner of the worst kind. I do not deserve freedom. I must atone; you do not understand. I thank you kindly but I must stay and take punishment for all the ill I have caused.'

'There is nothing worse than a repentant sinner,' complained Abraham in confused frustration. 'He must give up his evil ways and then be always reminding others of his faults. What is done is done, Preacher. The Lord Jehovah sees everything and will call on his reckoning in his good time. Now get on to those stables before I pin back thy ears with this stout rifle butt.'

Sullenly, Curly Bright obeyed, his mind in a ferment of indecision. 'I don't know,' he muttered. 'Dear Lord, guide my hand. Make clear my way, I beg of you.'

Roughly, Abraham tossed him up across the saddle. The brothers mounted and all three rode out slowly towards the closed main gates of the fort.

'Who goes?' called the gate guard.

'Open up,' replied Ezekiel, touching the peak of his forage cap with a saluting forefinger. 'Urgent dispatches travelling out.'

The guard peered at them in the gloom, 'What, three of you? Must be an awful lot of dispatches you got there.'

'Indeed it is, and most pressing too, so don't hesitate. We have ground to cover to north, south and west, so get those gates open now or answer to the captain of the guard.'

Complaining to himself at the late call, the gate guard called on a companion from the guardhouse. The two of them lifted the bar and slowly pushed the gates apart. Even before they were fully open Abraham squeezed through the gap and, with the others following, quickly rode off.

CHAPTER THIRTEEN

Buck Holdall and Lorn Chaser sat on horseback looking down at Kitty; they held a beaten and bloody Clay Rudebaugh propped up between them on his pinto.

'This here is yours I believe,' said Holdall, giving the dazed cowboy a booted shove that sent him tumbling from the saddle.

'What have you done?' cried Kitty, rushing forward to crouch over Clay.

'The boy came looking for trouble,' Holdall answered callously. 'He got what he asked for.'

Clay's face was a bruised mess; one eye was swollen shut and the other almost the same, his nose and lips were caked with dried blood. Kitty knelt beside him and lifted his head. 'Clay, can you hear me? What happened here?'

Clay tried to speak but only a husky whisper came from between his cracked lips.

'You beasts!' Kitty cried. 'How could you do such a thing?'

Holdall chuckled. 'Mighty easy, ma'am. And you can pass that little fact along to Jake Rains when you see him next.' His face tightened, 'We'll be looking to offer him some of the same.'

'Get out of here,' Kitty cried. 'Get off my property.'

'Well, here's the thing.' Holdall took out a ribbon-sealed, legal-looking document from his saddle-bag and waved it at her. 'See this, Miss Kitty? Us two here, we're now the duly elected bailiffs for the county. And it appears you're in default on your bank loan and they're foreclosing on you. Looks like you have to quit this place pronto or we have to come along and get you to leave, forcibly if need be.'

Kitty looked up at him aghast, 'You can't just throw me out.'

'Oh yes we can, ma'am. That's the law, y'see.'

'Is this Christopher Leeward's doing?' snapped Kitty. 'Because if it is, it's a mean and spiteful thing.'

'Couldn't say on that score, ma'am. Just doing our duty here.' Holdall's handsome face held a smug confidence that shifted sharply to narrow warning. 'You get your things together and be out of here by tomorrow, you hear?'

'But where will we go? This man's in a bad way.'

'Just be gone is all. And don't try your place in town neither, Mr Leeward needs the property back; he has other plans for it now.'

'You mean you'll force us out without a roof to go to? What kind of people are you?'

Holdall turned his horse, ready to leave. 'We're the law, lady. You get yourself gone now. Tomorrow we'll be back.'

'You wouldn't be doing this if Jake Rains were here,' snapped Kitty boldly.

Holdall turned back and rode over to her, cold menace in his voice.

'Why, yes we would, Miss Kitty. We'd take real kindly to discussing the matter with old Jake, that we would.' He turned to call over to Lorn Chaser. 'That's right, ain't it, Lorn?'

In way of answer, Chaser pointed his finger at Kitty and cocked back his thumb like a pistol. With a slow grin he bucked the digit. Snorting a laugh, Holdall tossed the foreclosure notice on the ground in front of Kitty and the two rode off.

Kitty cradled Clay's beaten head in her lap and watched them go. She rocked backwards and forwards on her heels in distress. 'What are we to do?' she sighed. 'Where are you, Jake? Oh, where are you now?'

CHAPTER FOURTEEN

Their departure had been well advertised and a great many city folk had lined the streets of Lincoln to see them off. A band had played rousing march tunes and children had run impishly amongst the crowd letting off firecrackers that startled mounted bystanders. The army had been forced to send along enlisted men to police the cheering crowd, which surged about in a boisterous atmosphere of holiday excitement more akin to the city's usual Arbor Day celebrations. It was a noisy, dazzling display of flag waving and noise and it stunned Jake and Sam, who were more used to the calm solitude of the open prairie than this kind of city mayhem. Brigadier Billy had taken it upon himself to start the race, which he did by dramatically firing his pistol in the air and gallantly waving his hat to urge them on.

It had begun well, with the two parties leaving side by side. Then, with a whoop and a holler, Jake and Sam had slapped their horses' rumps and set off at a bold run to take an early lead. Colonel Moodie sat in their dust, seriously intent over his steering arm while his two accompanying infantrymen passengers waved cheerily as they passed by the onlookers.

But that was far behind them now. The two mounts had proved good choices and the cowboys rode them in stages, much in the manner of the old Pony Express riders: dismounting every hour or so and running alongside to reduce the strain on the horses. Their opponents in the Phaeton were somewhere behind them when an explosive splutter caused the vehicle to swerve sideways and come to a sudden standstill at the roadside some five miles back.

'Looks like the colonel might be having a spot of trouble,' Sam said with a grin as they rode through the confines of a narrow draw.

Jake looked back over his shoulder and shrugged. 'Seems like it. Though sure is a pity we had to agree on following the roadway here. Cross-country would have been quicker.'

'Ach!' spat Sam. 'That machine can't keep up, no matter what the colonel says. To my way of thinking it'll never catch on, least-ways not out here.'

They dismounted again and walked alongside the ponies as they left the draw and a spread of wide countryside opened before them. The road ahead curved and followed a snaking path over a series of gently rolling hills that climbed into a higher range lying in the heat haze ahead. The sky was a clear blue and the scent of the open range, full of herbs and wild flowers growing amidst a carpet of bluestem grass, was in their nostrils. A meadowlark called warning and not far off a herd of white-tailed deer started at the sound.

'Feels good to be out here, don't it, Jake?' Sam smiled in contentment.

'Sure does. Don't think I could abide that city life. Felt like the whole place was about to come down on me.'

'Right enough, partner. You know, we should have taken a little side bet on the outcome of this here race. Could have earned us some running-around money.'

'Well,' said Jake guiltily. 'Reckon I did that already.'

'You did!' gasped Sam.

'Had a little personal agreement with the colonel there,' confessed Jake.

'Oh, my! Don't tell me you laid down the mustang money against us winning this race?'

Jake rubbed his jaw and glanced at Sam from under the brim of his campaign hat. 'Half of it, anyways.'

'That's a wild move, Jake.' Sam chuckled. 'Damn! I like it. We look to clean up here.'

'Sure as hell hope so. Barring accidents and God willing we might make us enough to set up Kitty with a fine herd of cows as well as a new barn.'

'You are the business, Jake. I never thought you'd take a chance like that, I swear I didn't.'

'Well.' Jake shrugged. 'You've got to speculate to accumulate. One of them city businessmen back there told me that. Seemed like good advice.'

That moonless night they rested off the road on slopes of the steep climb they had seen in the distance earlier. A small fire burned between them, and the ponies were hobbled and grazing near by. Jake was dozing peacefully when one of the horses whickered restlessly and woke him from his dreamy state. Sam was already on his feet. 'You hear that?' he asked.

'Damned if I do.'

It was the machine beat of the Phaeton echoing up to them; they could see the wavering beam of the vehicle's lamp some miles off bobbing and weaving along the road towards them in the darkness.

'Colonel got that thing going again and is looking to make up for lost time, it appears.'

'So it does,' agreed Jake, picking up his saddle and blanket. 'Maybe we'd best move on too.'

'Going to be tricky in the dark. Them ponies take a fall and we're out of the running.'

'It's a risk,' agreed Jake. 'But he hits the top of this rise before us and he'll sail on down the other side. We'll be hard put to outrun them then.'

'We'll make our time up at the river crossing, they've got to punt that thing across.'

'Best be sure,' said Jake, slapping the blanket across his pony.

'As you say,' Sam followed his lead and the two men mounted up.

Two hours later the Phaeton caught up with them as they crested the wide hilltop. Jake and Sam were forced to slow their pace to accommodate the incline in the dark, the rocky path being strewn with unseen loose shale. The colonel, though, threw caution to the wind and barrelled down the slope beside them, his passengers catcalling jeers as they passed in a whirl of noise and cloud of stones that caused the two ponies to whirl nervously.

'See you boys at the fort!' called the colonel, honking his horn derisively.

Grimly, Jake and Sam continued on, resisting the temptation to force the pace. 'We'll catch them at the river,' Sam repeated with unconvincing confidence.

As the dawn crept over the hilltop and cast deep shadows into the valley beyond they could see the horseless carriage on the bank of the river ford below. The river, a long gleam of coiling silver in the cold light, was not deep enough to impede swimming ponies, but was too deep for the four-wheeled vehicle to make it across. The colonel and his men were knee deep in the shallows, struggling to manhandle the machine onto a lashed pole raft. The vehicle had canted to one side and one wheel hung over the edge of the raft. The machine was in danger of being tipped into the slow-moving water.

'Let's go, Sam,' said Jake, laying the spur to his pony, which leapt forward down the slope in a muscle-bunched run.

With a whoop of excitement Sam followed on behind, and in minutes the two reached the riverbank to pull up in a flurry of mud alongside the Phaeton.

'Good day to you, gentlemen,' called Jake as he surged on into the water without pause.

The three army men watched him pass with sour expressions on their faces. They were soaked through and plastered with mud. 'I'll catch you yet, Jake Rains,' the colonel called after then.

'Well, it's sink or swim, Colonel. And I do declare it looks like you're about to do the former,' Jake replied. He dropped back over his pony's rump and caught its tail as the beast's hoofs left the riverbed and began swimming.

'There's still a way to go, Jake,' shouted the colonel after him. 'This race is far from over.'

Jake and Sam climbed the far riverbank and without pausing to dry off kept up a fast pace, letting the rising sun steam off their soaked clothes. At the next rise Jake pulled up to look back. He saw that the Phaeton was now safely mounted on the raft and the three men were poling it across the river. 'Keep pushing, Sam,' cried Jake. 'We need to make a good lead.'

In reply, Sam lashed at his pony with his reins and they both pounded on. The creatures surged away, their earlier rest paying off dividends as they ran at full speed and with an obvious natural enjoyment at the run.

The Macafees waited.

They had chosen their hiding-place well. Though they remained unseen from afar, their view along the approach road was clear for miles. The two brothers sat in sombre silence on either side of a high narrow pass. They were patient hunters, used to long waits without movement or thought and they settled in passively, their long rifles ready beside them. Only Curly Bright fretted, his inner churnings causing him to twitch with distress.

The Macafees had set him in plain view, sitting on a rock at the roadside and early passing travellers had looked at the troubled man with concern. Some asked if he was alright, thinking some mishap had befallen him, but Curly Bright just shook his head and waved them on. He knew the men who were hidden in the rocks on either side and what they were capable of. If any paused to help him they might well fall prey to the merciless guns of the Macafees.

Set high up, the Macafees chosen ambush overlooked, on one side, a steep rock-strewn ravine, whilst the approach road led up from the level plains below and climbed around large scattered granite boulders, some as big as a two-storey house. The first hint that Jake and Sam received of anything amiss was the warning offered by the good samaritan who had passed Curly Bright earlier. He called out to the two riders as they passed him.

'Mind how you go ahead. There's some crazy loon sitting up there in the pass.'

The two cowboys were riding fast and only caught the man's words on the wind as they rode quickly by him. It took a while for the warning to sink in, but when it did Jake searched the road ahead carefully.

'You see anything, Sam?' he asked, as they slowed to a walk.

Sam squinted at the distant narrow pass, 'There's something there. I see a man, I think.'

'Fellow we just passed said he was a crazy.'

'Looks as if he's just setting there.'

'Maybe nothing,' Jake shrugged, urging his pony on again.

'No crime in taking a rest, I guess.'

They rode on and as they came nearer to the base of the steep incline Jake could feel a sense of unease creeping over him. It was an old instinct and not one he was given to ignoring.

'Something ain't right, Sam.'

'Yeah,' Sam agreed. 'I get it too. Maybe we should step out a mite on foot.'

'Hold on, I'll take a look through my binoculars.' They dismounted and Jake unpacked the glasses from his saddlebags; they were a standard issue and had come along with the borrowed equipment. With them, Jake took a steadying stance over his saddle horn and focused in on the distant figure of the sitting man.

'Mighty sad-looking fellow,' he said. 'You know, if I didn't know better I'd swear that was Curly Bright Smith setting there. Here Sam, you take a look.'

'Can't be,' said Sam, reaching across to take the binoculars. 'They got him held in—'

The binoculars flew apart in the space between them, becoming a twisted piece of metal and shattered glass that splintered in a sudden explosion as it flew out of Jake's hand. Then they heard the sound: the boom of the long rifle and the high looping hum of the bullet. Instinctively the two dived sideways as a second bullet hummed into the space they had just occupied. Scrabbling on all fours, Jake burrowed off to the left, seeking cover from the boulders, whilst Sam did the same off to the right.

'The hell is that?' called Sam.

'Bushwhackers,' Jake said. 'That's a long-range rifle. Could be a Sharps.'

'You don't think. . . ?' Sam left the question hanging.

'I reckon,' Jake answered grimly. 'Those Macafees are out of jail. It has to be them, the only two I know who've got it in for us and carry buffalo guns.'

Their two ponies had turned away at the confusion and wandered off, the rifles in their scabbards now being too far away to reach safely. Another shot whined off the rock face above Jake's head, blowing a cascade of chips over him. 'They got us pinned down right and proper,' Jake said, sucking at his palm where the destroyed binoculars had taken a hunk of flesh with them. Flapping his hand to cool off the burn, Jake drew his pistol from its box holster. It was the Mauser C96 that he favoured, the broomhandle model with a magazine of ten rounds set in front of the trigger guard. A foot long and weighing three and a half pounds, it was not a quick-draw weapon and, although a mite nose heavy, with due compensation this German-made Obendorf Factory piece had stood him in good stead for accuracy up until now. Still, he looked after his wandering horse with disappointment; at this distance he could certainly do with that rifle right now; he wondered whether he should chance it.

As if reading his thoughts a shot cracked out and dropped the pony as suddenly as if its legs had been swept away. Another followed and Sam's horse went the same way, killed instantly by the powerful gun.

Sam drew his six-shooter out and looked across at Jake with a question in his raised eyebrows: *what do we do now?*

Jake shrugged in reply: *I don't know.*

The pair of Sharps boomed with regularity, the .40-calibre shells chipping fountains of earth or stone from all around the two men as they huddled behind their sparse cover. It was beginning to remind Jake of an earlier time, when he had waited at the foot of Kettle Hill ready for the charge up that hellish climb in Cuba, although these were no poorly trained Spanish infantrymen up above but two wily and experienced sharpshooters who had held a rifle in their hands as soon as they could stand. Not only that, they were also armed with the most accurate distance firearm of modern times.

Jake really did not want a repeat of the Cuban experience as he looked across at Sam, thinking sadly of his other friend, Calum Cartright, and how it had ended for him. It seemed there was no alternative though; if they were to survive they had to go above and winkle the Macafees out from their hiding-places. Then he heard the booming voice of Abraham echoing down to him.

'How art thee this day, Brother Rains? Ready to stand and fight yet? Look ye here, we have brought thy friend Curly Bright Smith before thee.'

Jake took off his hat and peeked around the edge of his covering boulder. He saw Curly Bright, standing now in the roadway, head raised skywards and hands crossed on his chest as he sought divine guidance.

'Come save him, Jake Rains. And you, Samuel, have ye no enmity left for thy brother's slayer? Ye forgave him, they say. What manner of man art thee? A coward, I say. Wilt let a man take thy brother's life and think no more of it? Well, I am not like thee, Samuel Parks. Blood for blood, I say and so it will be. Come on, Samuel Parks, come try me, if ye dare.'

Jake could see that Sam was fuming at the taunt and he called across, 'Cool down, Sam. They want you acting rash.'

125

'I know it,' growled Sam. 'I ain't going nowhere, don't you worry. Leastways not just yet awhile.'

The two turned as they heard the puttering clatter of the approaching Phaeton behind them and turned to see the colonel in his horseless carriage, roaring down towards them along the road. Both his soldier passengers had rifles ready and it was obvious that they had heard the shooting and had come poste-haste on a rescue mission. Jake shook his head sadly. They were sitting ducks on the open road and although he tried to wave them off, Jake could see the colonel, eyes bright and teeth bared as he drove blindly forward with all the wild courage of a man leading a cavalry charge.

The speeding vehicle was almost level with Jake and Sam when two shots from the Sharps boomed out simultaneously. The carriage took the heavy-calibre rounds, one slamming in between the colonel's legs and passing right through the metal floor, the other ricocheting off the wheel shaft, skewing the forward axle and bending both wheels inwards.

The carriage cartwheeled, sending its passengers flying as it crashed forward in a cloud of dust. It rolled in a bouncing run, crushing the leather cover and shedding pieces of metal trim as it went. The machine slid along with a metallic shriek and ended upside down in the middle of the road. The wreck rested momentarily amidst a dusty cloud, ticking ominously and dripping gasoline from its shattered tank. Then in a voluminous explosion the reserve gasoline cans caught fire. A sheet of bright flame shot skywards, accompanied by a tremendous explosion that blew the remains of the machine apart in flaming shards.

The dazed survivors scrabbled to find cover, the colonel sliding down beside Jake whilst the two soldiers made it over alongside Sam.

'We heard the shooting way back,' panted the colonel. 'What is it, road agents?'

'Worse,' answered Jake. 'Two mean old sharpshooters who have a bone to pick with us.'

The colonel looked over sadly at his wrecked vehicle. 'Well, they've already cost me a goodly sum and that's a fact.'

'Afraid it looks like our little race is over,' Jake observed wryly.

'Let's hope we get out of this to try again,' said the colonel with a grin. He was obviously starting to enjoy the whole affair. 'So can we have a status report, Mr Rains?'

'Yes sir,' said Jake falling naturally into his old military style. 'Two sharpshooters armed with Sharps rifles. Keen shots and not to be taken at all for granted. They have a hostage up there, one Curly Bright Smith, an old time outlaw turned preacher. We have more men than them just now but they hold the high ground and have range on us, those rifles are good for a thousand yards.'

'I see,' said the colonel, peering cautiously around the covering boulder. 'Well, it's a frontal attack, plain and simple as I see it. It's a fair climb but spread out we offer fewer targets. Best of it is at least there's some cover for us on the way up.'

'It's a long haul up there, Colonel.'

'Nothing ventured, nothing gained, Mr Rains,' the colonel answered boldly. He waved across at his men. 'Spread out, boys. We'll take these rascals down or I'll want to know why. Let's to it!'

The men obediently began to climb upward, moving cautiously in crouching runs and keeping as many of the large boulders between them and the shooters as they possibly could. Sam and Jake followed the colonel's lead, zigzagging behind as the Sharps barked noisily above them sending down a steady rain of lead.

Curly Bright meanwhile struggled internally. He was angry, an emotion he had suppressed for many years. Now he argued with the rising wave, condemning the unsought feelings with prayers to his Creator and wondering which path he should follow. It was a wrench; he had felt more than able to take the punishment legally meted out to him for all his past crimes, but even so the thought of being a part of this ambuscade troubled him. He sat at a loss, a lone figure on his rock whilst bullets whizzed about him. Ignoring the gun battle he clenched his fists and fumed in indecision.

Jake, Sam and the others had made it halfway up the slope when one of the soldiers took a hit and was thrown full length on his back. Sam dragged him to cover and saw he had taken a flesh wound along the ribs. He pulled off the man's bandanna, bunched it and advised the soldier to keep it pressed hard against the wound to stanch the blood flow, with the assurance that he was not too badly wounded. Then Sam was off again, firing as he went. They had no easy targets but at least they reasoned that a steady course of fire would keep the heads of the Macafees down.

Jake was hugging the girth of a huge boulder and reloading the Mauser magazine from his cartridge belt. He was wondering how long his ammunition would last when the battle took a turn.

Curly Bright finally snapped. He could find no answer in his prayers and the whirl of gunfire penetrated through his cloud of confusion. He reasoned that if God would not take a hand then he must take it upon himself to fight the good fight. He was unarmed but the nearest Macafee to him was Ezekiel, who was kneeling on the steep side of the road behind a spread of rocks as he potted at the men below.

With an unthinking bellow, Curly Bill launched himself at the backwoodsman and in a flying charge caught the surprised man in the circle of his spread arms. The two of them fell in a tangle. Ezekiel was impeded by his damaged leg and trapped in a refusal to part with his long rifle, which he swung up in an attempt to crack Curly Bright's skull. Curly Bright caught the glancing blow which rattled off the side of his temple but Ezekiel's raised arms enabled Curly Bright to deliver a hefty fist to his stomach. Ezekiel doubled over, winded, and Curly Bright was on him quickly, laying down heavy punches as he straddled the Macafee in an almost demented attack.

Abraham turned, catching sight of the movement at Ezekiel's position. He swung his rifle round but was fearful of hitting his brother, so he held his fire, waiting until the two wrestling men parted. At this interruption to the firing the men below covered good ground on their climb.

'We have them,' panted the red-faced and sweating colonel, whose earlier enthusiasm was waning as his breath gave out. He was no longer the sprightly young lieutenant he had once been and the climb had proved more taxing that he had bargained for.

'Not yet,' answered Jake, launching himself upwards in a reckless run. 'But something's distracting them. Better make the most of it.' He broke free of the concealing boulders and as he covered the remaining yards he saw at a glance what was going on. Curly Bright and Ezekiel struggled on the brink of the shale loaded drop whilst Abraham raised himself and angled his Sharps, hoping for a clear shot. Curly Bright, now free of his somewhat overzealous religious restrictions and unlocking the killer that still lurked deep inside him, pummelled the semiconscious Ezekiel, sitting astride his chest and delivering blow after blow on the Macafee's bloody face. With a wild look of blank rage, Curly Bright finally let up his blows and climbed off. With the obvious intention of pushing the Macafee over he hauled Ezekiel to the edge of the drop by the collar of his buckskin shirt.

At last Abraham had his clear shot at the standing figure heaving at his brother. He pulled the trigger. At the same moment Jake shouted a warning, firing on the run. The semiautomatic Mauser pumped shot after shot at the exposed kneeling figure of Abraham who buckled, his Sharps spinning from his grip. It was too late for Curly Bright though, who took the heavy-gauge round through his side and flopped limply over the edge of the cliff, his hand still firmly locked in Ezekiel's collar. The two of them disappeared over, the one pulled by the weight of the other. There was a rattle of stones and they were gone from sight.

Jake, gun held ready, stood over the figure of Abraham who lay sprawled amongst the rocks. Blood ran from the corner of his mouth and into his beard as he looked up at Jake with barely focused eyes.

'Curse you, Rains, ye've done for me,' he husked, before his eyes, fixed in a stare of bestial hatred, glazed over for all eternity.

Sam was looking down into the ravine as Jake walked over and joined him. Behind them, the remaining rifleman was helping the now exhausted colonel up the last few steps of the climb.

'Wondered why they held off,' Sam said, looking down at the two crumpled bodies lying amongst the rocks far below. 'Thought maybe they ran out of ammo.'

'Looks like Curly Bright decided to take a hand here and save our bacon,' Jake observed.

'And Abraham?' asked Sam, jerking his chin in the direction of the older Macafee.

'Right now he's finding out what really lies 'twixt heaven and hell.'

'Guess I know which way he'll be heading.'

'Maybe so,' Jake agreed. He took out his tobacco pouch and began to roll a spill.

'Now what?' asked Sam.

Slowly, Jake lit up and took a long draw. 'Guess we walk.'

CHAPTER FIFTEEN

Kitty spooned some more soup into Clay Rudebaugh's mouth. His lobsided lips dribbled some onto his chin and Kitty patiently wiped it away with a cloth.

'Right sorry, Miss Kitty,' slurred Clay. 'I'm afraid my mouth ain't working too good these days.'

Clay had not recovered well from his beating at the hands of Leeward's gunmen and shortly afterwards he had suffered a stroke that left one side of his face frozen and the loss of the use of his left arm. Kitty insisted he rest until he was fully recovered and that she would tend to him during his convalescence.

'Think no more of it, Clay. Just you get yourself well,' she said, offering him another spoonful.

'Bless you, m'am. You're a real angel of mercy.'

Kitty no longer looked an angel of any sort. Driven from her home she had been forced to use the last few dollars of her meagre savings to purchase an old patched canvas Conestoga wagon that had fared better when it had crossed the country in the settling days fifty years earlier. The team that came with the wagon had been no better, poor nags that were on their last legs but all that Kitty could afford. The two of them now inhabited the wagon alongside the few possessions Kitty had been able to save from the ranch before Buck Holdall and Lorn Chaser had forcibly evicted her.

Her once finely coiffed golden hair was now in disarray, unwashed, ratty and tied back in a bunch with twine. Her few items of decent wardrobe suffered from the outdoor life they led and were crumpled, dusty and worn. Mostly now she wore blue jeans and a workshirt and even they had seen better days. There was little opportunity to bathe and the two of them suffered from the lack of cleanliness as result; this was a particular hardship that was difficult for Kitty to bear. Perpetually grimy and sore, Kitty drove the wagon towards Fort Brill, hoping to make contact with Jake or at least discover what had happened to him. It was a long, slow process, the poor team struggling hard to pull the heavy wagon along, and Kitty prayed that they would not drop in their traces before they reached the fort.

Oakum now lived under a reign of terror in which Leeward fulfilled his egocentric sense of power. If anything it had unhinged him to some degree and he carried on as if he were a king, ordering the populace to bend to his will, partly by the use of civic ordinances from his mayoral office and also by fear-instilled pressure from his team of gunmen. In consequence Kitty had been unable to find help from her neighbours as Leeward had seen to it that she was hounded from pillar to post by his henchmen. Any amongst the townspeople who offered to help were dissuaded by the threat of violence. His plan was to drive her to such a state that she would come begging for his help and with magnanimous generosity from his newly found status he would condescend to take her as wife and, as he would have it, his slave.

Kitty had been forced to cross the county line to be able to buy the wagon and it was from there that she made her way back to the main trail north. They lived off the land as best they could; luckily there was plenty of wildlife and Kitty's prowess with the rifle stood them in good stead, with rabbit, quail and deer falling under her gun.

But it was a tiring process for a woman, hunting and caring for an invalid, unused as she was to such a physical life and the strain began to show in her sun-reddened features with the advent of lines where none had been before.

She cleaned up after feeding Clay, made sure the horses were cared for and, taking up the Winchester, she poked her head in at the back of the wagon. 'I'll take a turn at picking up a few cottontails for the pot, OK, Clay? Be back in a while.'

'Sure thing, Miss Kitty,' the cowhand replied from inside the wagon. 'You take care. Sure wish I was up to helping out. Feel like some poor baby child here, being so helpless and all.'

'Don't you think on it; you'll be up and about helping out real soon, I'm sure.'

'I danged well hope so,' Clay said with obvious frustration.

'Rest easy, see you soon.'

Kitty made her way to the nearby knoll where ash, elm and hackberry grew in profusion. She knew it would be a good spot for rabbit, she had seen the white tails bouncing around in the distance from their campsite. She entered the shade of the trees and stood awhile, enjoying the serene sound of the breeze rustling through the leaves above her. The peace gave her a moment of repose and she closed her eyes, leaning back against a trunk and letting the stress slide off her as if she stood under the fresh water of a spring rainfall.

The soft voice, when it came, startled her and she jumped, bringing up the rifle quickly.

'Howdy, Miss Kitty.'

Buck Holdall's fist clenched firmly over the rifle barrel and with a smug grin on his face he wrenched it from her grasp. 'Now, you won't be needing that.'

The crouching figure of Lorn Chaser moved silently from behind the dark shadow of another tree, a thin smile showing beneath his stone-dead eyes.

'Where you a-going, Miss Kitty? Ain't right a widow woman being out here all alone,' Buck smarmed. 'Well, leastways with only the company of a busted-up old cripple, that is.'

'You. . . !' gasped Kitty. 'You stay away from me.'

'We been watching you, lady,' Buck continued. 'You and that useless cowhand you got there in the wagon. Seems you could do with a little help here. Mr Leeward now, he told us to come looking for you, see if we could offer some assistance.'

'I . . . I don't want your help. Just leave us be.'

'Can't do that, m'am. Mr Leeward says to bring you back to Oakum and that's what we aim to do.'

'I don't want to go back there.'

Buck grabbed her tightly by the arm and leaned his face near.

'Well, you're going back, like it or not, Miss High and Mighty. Think you're too good for the likes of us, don't you? Leeward'll teach you a lesson or two on that score. Now, get along back to the wagon.' With that he shoved her roughly forward in front of him whilst Lorn Chaser followed behind, leading their horses.

They reached the wagon and Buck went straight to the tail and leant in.

'How're you, Clay? Feeling a mite poorly I hear.'

Clay leapt nervously at sight of his face. He tried to lean over and reach his gunbelt, but his actions were pathetically limited and he knew it was useless. Buck hopped up into the wagon and snatched up the gunbelt. He leant over the helpless man and sneered down at him. 'Better off you was dead and gone, Clay Rudebaugh. You ain't no use to anyone no more.'

'Leave him alone!' screamed Kitty from outside, as she struggled to free herself from Lorn Chaser's grip. 'Don't you hurt him any more.'

Buck's face appeared at the canvas door. 'Oh, I ain't going to harm him, Miss Kitty. We're going to leave him right where he is. That's right, ain't it Lorn?'

Lorn nodded and tugged Kitty away as Buck climbed back down. 'Now you get along and cut one of those sorry-looking nags out to ride back with us,' ordered Buck. 'We'll just wait on you here. No rush, we got plenty of time. Don't you think on running off though, will you? Those spavined creatures won't make it far without us catching up to you, and that's a fact.'

Sullenly, Kitty obeyed, her mind racing as to some means of escape. But there was none. They were right: she could not make a run for it. There was only miles of open countryside to cross with a sorry horse under her. They would catch up to her easily.

She took the fittest of the team and fashioned a bridle from a length of leather trace rein. She led it back to the wagon, climbed up a few wheel spokes to clamber aboard and ride the creature bareback.

'That's it.' Buck smiled from where he leant against the wagon boards, watching her. 'You sure are turning into a frontierswoman, Miss Kitty.'

'What about Clay?' she asked. 'We can't just leave him here.'

'Why the hell not?' asked Buck as he mounted up. 'He's no use to the rest of us now anyhow.'

'But that's inhuman. He can't fend for himself, he'll starve out here all alone. Please, bring him along. I'll care for him. He'll be no trouble to you.'

'Sure,' Buck nodded. 'Now you just do as I say and get on. We don't have no time for no cripples.'

With that, he whirled his pony and smacked the rump of Kitty's mount, urging it on. Buck gave Lorn a nod as he followed after her. 'Get rid of the rest of those nags. There might be more life in old Clay than he lets on.'

Kitty spun around at sound of the shots as Lorn Chaser obediently felled the remainder of the team. 'I'll send help, Clay!' she called. 'Somehow or other, I'll send help.'

In truth Kitty knew it was empty encouragement; in her heart she guessed there would be little chance that she would be able to do anything to aid the helpless man left alone in the isolated wagon.

CHAPTER SIXTEEN

Jake was glad to be back on Penny and it seemed the mare was happy about it too. Normally a stand-offish beast with an obvious high opinion of herself, it seemed that her spell in the cavalry stables at Fort Brill had made the creature appreciate the attention that Jake gave to her. She nuzzled up to him at first sight and could not wait to be free of the crowded stables.

'There's a sight,' Jake said to Sam as they trotted along side by side.

'What, your mare?'

'Look at this.' Jake smiled. 'Usually I get the ornery treatment the minute I put the saddle on. Now she can't wait to be moving along.'

'Maybe you treat her too good,' observed Sam.

Jake leant down and patted Penny's neck.

'No, I don't think so. She's just got a character all her own. Ain't you, girl?'

Sam smiled, 'You sure know how to treat a lady, Jake.'

'Aw, don't know about that. I never been much of a hand with the womenfolk.'

'Well, you ready to take a bit of advice from an older man?'

'Sure. What's that?'

'I seen the way Miss Kitty looks at you. You could do a lot worse, Jake Rains.'

Jake looked at him and then away quickly as something caught in his throat. 'You think so?' he said doubtfully.

'Damned right I do.'

After purchasing a ride on a loaded supply wagon for the price of a couple of Sharps rifles, the party had arrived safely back at the fort. The wounded soldier was hurried to the infirmary and the colonel promised to see them as soon as he had made a telegraph report to the brigadier back in Lincoln.

True to his word, once Jake and Sam had bathed and had a meal, a crestfallen colonel called them in.

'Well,' he confessed. 'Brigadier Billy wasn't too pleased. Seems like our mechanized army might have to take a back seat for a while. He didn't like the notion of the gasoline going off like that, felt it might be a touch too dangerous. Bullets and inflammables don't mix in his opinion.'

'Might be he has a point,' Jake agreed.

'Still though,' the colonel shook his head, 'I'm convinced there's a way forward in this. We'll just have to wait and see.'

'You about to invest in another one of those horseless carriages, Colonel?' Sam asked.

The colonel shook his head. 'Not at that price. But look, fellows, I just wanted to thank you for going along with it all. Mighty sporting of you. Are you headed home now?'

'Sure are,' said Jake. 'We've been away a little too long. They'll be worrying where we've got to back there.'

'Well, Godspeed and when you get some more mustangs you bring them along, you hear?'

On that note they had collected their stored gear and set off on the road back to Oakum. Both were eager to get back to the ranch and see how the other two had fared. Jake could not wait to see Kitty's face when he unloaded the cash in his saddlebags. He knew it would inspire them all with hope for the future. That and the promise of a ready market for more mustang remounts for the army.

When they were a day out from Oakum the two cowboys camped for the night a little off the main trail. They stopped in a clearing amongst forest trees and as Sam unloaded their gear,

Jake went off to find dry wood for a fire. He was about to return when he saw a flash of white through the trees. The moon was up and the whiteness seemed unnatural under the bright light. Jake set aside the brushwood he had collected and carefully made his way towards the sheen of white. He parted some brush and found himself in an open field with a wagon standing there. He could see the carcasses of dead horses and felt the air of desolation about the place. Something bad had happened here, he reasoned.

He drew the Mauser and made his way over to the wagon, not quite knowing what to expect. Looking inside he could make out the outline of a figure lying there. A lamp hung from the doorway and he struck a match and lit it. By its brightness, Jake saw the bandaged figure of Clay Rudebaugh. At sight of the cowboy, Jake's heart sunk. Quickly he climbed up into the wagon bed. He leant down and could hear Clay's ragged breath. The man was still alive.

There was a canteen near by but it had been drained dry. Jake shook the man, 'Clay! Clay! Can you hear me?'

His only answer was a vague murmur from the prone figure. Jake hesitated no longer: he jumped from the wagon and ran through the trees to fetch Sam and the horses.

Later when they had a fire going, they brought Clay out of the wagon and laid him alongside the warmth. Jake wet the man's lips and let him drink frugally from his canteen.

'What the hell happened here?' asked Sam.

'I don't know but those dead horses yonder don't bode well.'

'You think Miss Kitty's alright?'

Jake looked at him over the firelight and Sam could see the obvious worry. Jake bit his lip, 'I've a mind to ride on and find out.'

'Now steady on,' warned Sam. 'Let's just see what Clay says. Could be he's just quit the ranch and taken up carting, then fell amongst thieves.'

'Look at him, Sam. There's no way he could drive a wagon;

he's been beat up too bad.'

Jake splashed water liberally over Clay's face. 'Come on, boy. Wake up. You've got to tell us what happened.'

Clay gasped, his eyelids fluttering at the sudden cool rush. 'What? I ain't dreaming, am I? Is that you, Jake, Sam? How in all that's holy did you get here?' His voice was slurred and slow but he was aware at last.

'You ain't dreaming, partner,' said Sam softly. 'How'd you come to this pretty pass?'

'Them two riders of Leeward's, they took Miss Kitty and left me for dead.'

As his head cleared, Jake lifted the man up and propped him against his bent knee. 'Thanks boys,' said Clay. 'I was sure I was a goner. Once the water ran out I thought that was it, I was about ready to cash in my chips about now.'

Jake allowed him some more water from the canteen. 'That's it, slowly does it, Clay. Not too much too quick.'

Clay nodded his thanks and wiped his mouth with the back of his good hand. 'Afraid it's been a bad time since you fellows left,' he explained. 'Leeward foreclosed on Miss Kitty and threw her off the ranch. He had his boys beat me up and I ain't been right since, my arm's dead and my face don't work to well either. I couldn't do a thing to stop them. I'm real sorry, boys.'

Jake and Sam tutted. 'Don't think on it, Clay. That's right bad luck for you. Where'd they take Miss Kitty?'

'She was a real angel, Jake. She took me on and nursed me even though she didn't have nothing left. Can't say I've ever seen a woman with such spirit. Not in all my days. Those scoundrels took her off back to Oakum. Back to Leeward; he wouldn't let her go.'

Jake leant back, his eyes fixed on the flames. Sam watched him and could see the anger rising as Jake's fists clenched. 'Easy, boy. Easy,' said Sam softly. 'Think on it. Work it through. Don't go off half-cocked.'

'I made a promise, Sam,' Jake hissed. 'I made a promise to

139

care for her. Gave my word on it.'

'I know, I know, and we'll see she's alright. We'll do that but we have to work out how.'

'They've taken over the town,' Clay cut in. 'That Cole Reichter is the sheriff now. Leeward fooled folks and got himself made mayor, then he gave Miss Kitty's ranch to those other two, Holdall and Chaser.'

'What happened to Sheriff Deeling?' asked Sam.

'Found backshot on the road out of town.'

'Got to have been Leeward's bunch. They'd be real good at that.'

'They're going to die for this,' Jake snarled with quiet menace. 'All of them. If it's the last thing I do.'

'They got the law on their side though,' said Clay. 'That's the problem you've got to face; they did everything with a legal seal on it.'

'Don't matter to me,' said Jake with finality. 'Their day is done.'

'You want to end up like me, Jake?' said Sam. 'Running all your days? It has to look right or you'll have the law on your tail.'

Jake laid Clay back down gently, then he got up and looked steadily at Sam. 'You speak reason, I know, Sam. And I hear you, but I'm going to finish that scum come hell or high water. So, I ain't talking on it any more. Come first light I'm going in there and if I see any one of them on the street . . . he's a dead man.'

By the next dawn, Jake had calmed down considerably. He saw the sense in what Sam had said, it would not help Kitty if he rode in solely intent on murder. She was his first priority. He had to make sure she was safe before taking any other action.

Sam awoke to see Jake hunched over the fire, his figure an unmoving silhouette against the dawn light. Sam tossed off his blanket and got up. 'You got coffee there?' he asked.

'Sure, help yourself.'

'How's Clay doing?' Sam asked, pouring himself a steaming mug.

'Better. He just needed some water; he's been sleeping like a baby.'

'That's good. How about you, partner?'

Jake looked across at Sam. 'It's right, what you said. I've been thinking it through. We have to get Kitty out first.'

Sam nodded, 'Makes sense. You've obviously been figuring. What did you come up with?'

'Well, first off we have to know where she is. In the town or out at his ranch. Oakum's laid out in that valley with forested slopes, it shouldn't be too difficult for us to slide in there and keep watch on the town. See who goes where.'

'Now you're thinking right,' Sam approved. 'Can't do nothing without a plan.'

'The way I see it, to avoid any comeback we have to get a confession out of one of them. We need one alive to tell it all before a court. Our best bet is Reichter, he's the weakest.'

'I agree. Just a bully boy who'll fold like a pack of cards once the pressure is on.'

'So we isolate him right off. Keep him somewhere safe until it's all over.'

'Well, he's sitting in the jailhouse. Could be the right place for him to stay locked up.' Jake smiled at the notion, 'That's fine. Now what do we do about Clay here?'·

'I hear you,' said Clay, sitting up and wide awake. 'I've been listening. You can count me in. Nothing I'd like better than to nursemaid that no-account Reichter.'

'Can you handle it, Clay?' asked Sam doubtfully.

Clay frowned at them with grim determination, 'I got one good hand. You set me up with a double barrel and I'll hold it steady on that mother's son.'

Jake and Sam laughed at the little man's grit, 'You sure got some sand, Clay.'

'I owe it. Personally, I'd like nothing better than to take down them fellows one and all but seeing how I'm fixed right now, that's going to have to be your score to settle.'

By the time night had arrived the three men had reached the town and lay in hiding at the edge of the forest above Oakum. The streets below glowed mellow under the lamplight but there were few people about. There was a stillness about the town that gave a slightly unsettling air. Jake remembered his first sight of the place and how his impressions had altered since then. It had looked like a sweet place to be back then. Now something dark and oppressive hung over the town, but Jake was sure it could be sweet again; there just had to be a little selective weeding done to clean the place up.

'How do you think the townsfolk will be?' Jake asked Clay, who seemed much refreshed after the ride down doubled up with Sam. 'Will they help?'

'They've had enough of Leeward's high-and-mighty ways all right,' Clay said. 'Whether they'll run to shooting it out with him, that I doubt. He's got them all scared for their lives. They're mostly peaceable folk, unused to the gun.'

Jake nodded; he turned to Sam, who had a pair of binoculars fixed to his face. 'You see anything?'

'I see Reichter. He's just left the saloon, he's on his way over to the sheriff's office now.'

'Any of the others?'

'Haven't seen sight of them at all.'

'Could be they're out of town,' said Clay.

'Could be,' agreed Jake. 'We'll give it another few minutes. Then if nothing happens we'll go down and take Reichter.'

Cole Reichter wallowed in his self-importance. He liked the way people stepped aside when he passed by. The crowd in the Barrel of Beer all offered him deference now, making way for him at the bar as he set up a tab he never intended to pay off. He could drink all he liked, eat all he liked and nobody dared say a word to him. It was the kind of power he had sought after all his life and now it pleasured him mightily to have finally achieved it.

Contentedly he plunked himself down comfortably in his office chair and slid out a bottle for one last noggin before bed. He had taken to sleeping on a bunk in one of the cells out back; although he already had a room over at the stage stopover he was often either too drunk or too lazy to walk there.

Burping gently, he uncorked the bottle and began pouring himself a shot. He started as the door suddenly opened and whiskey splashed over the desktop.

'What the. . . ?' he began angrily, looking up at the two characters who stood in the doorway silhouetted against the streetlight.

'Evening, Sheriff,' said Jake, bringing his Mauser into plain view.

'Rains!' gasped Reichter. 'What the hell are you doing here?'

'Right,' said Jake, pushing the door wide as he and Sam entered. 'Should be dead meat, shouldn't we? Dead by the Macafees' hand if you had your way. Dead like poor old Sheriff Deeling, shot down on the road going about his business.'

'Now, wait on,' said Reichter, nervously raising his hands at sight of the guns. His voice trembled a little as the door was slammed shut behind Sam. 'Just wait just a minute.'

'Why should we waste a second on the likes of you?' asked Sam, clicking back the hammer on his revolver.

'Let up now, boys. This ain't right. I'm peace officer here,' Reichter blustered noisily. 'You can't come on in here and threaten me like this. It'll go bad for you.'

'Don't mean squat to us, Reichter,' Jake snapped, raising the Mauser straight up and pointing at the sheriff's face. 'Where's Kitty Cartright?'

'I . . . I. . . .' mumbled Reichter.

'Spit it out, Sheriff. Before I plug you where you sit.'

'She's with Leeward, out at his place,' Reichter gushed. 'Look, you don't have to do this. I didn't mean you fellows no harm.'

'And the other two, Holdall and Chaser?'

'At the old Cartright place. They. . .' he paused. 'They own it now,' he finished limply.

'Not for long,' promised Jake.

Jake and Sam moved closer to Reichter, standing over him in a threatening manner. Sam reached down and hoisted the pistol from the sheriff's holster. Reichter's face crumpled, 'Wh . . . what you going to do to me?'

'What do you think?' Jake answered coldly.

'Look, don't do it. Please don't. I'll do anything. Really I will,' Reichter begged, all semblance of his earlier bravado gone.

'You've got one chance, Reichter. One chance to live.'

Reichter was beginning to shake uncontrollably, 'What is it? Tell me and it's done.'

'Can you write?' asked Jake.

Reichter shook his head sorrowfully.

'Dumb as well as ugly,' observed Sam.

'I can tell it,' cried Reichter plaintively. 'Whatever you want, I can tell it.'

'That you will,' promised Jake. 'You're going to tell it all. How Leeward has run this place. How he finagled the ranch away from Kitty Cartright. Who it was killed Sheriff Deeling—'

'It was them other two,' Reichter barked suddenly and a little too quickly. 'I had nothing to do with it.'

Sam glanced across at Jake as he read the truth in Reichter's hurried words. 'So it was you,' he said. 'You're the one. A back-shooter too, you murderous little tyke.'

'Leeward made me do it,' blubbered Reichter. 'He made me.'

'Get up and get in there.' Jake waved his gun barrel at the door to the cells.

'What? I told you I'll tell everything. Don't hurt me.'

'You're going into one of your own cages, you sack of grease,' snapped Jake, nodding at Sam, who opened the door and let Clay hobble in.

'Howdy, Sheriff.' Clay grinned and took one look at the shivering man. He made for the gun rack to take down a shotgun

144

with his good hand. 'You and me going to spend some time together. Now I don't operate so well at the moment. Fingers gets a little twitchy now and then, so you'll have to excuse me. Sudden movements. They get me all het up, you understand?'

Reichter looked Clay up and down nervously before stumbling over to the cells, his hands held high.

'Where to first. Leeward or the others?' asked Sam as they left the sheriff's office.

'I have to get Kitty safe.'

'Then it's the L double E.'

They took up position in the same copse of trees they had occupied before which, gave them a good overview of the ranch. Nothing stirred below and all was dark in the main house.

'Pretty peaceful,' whispered Sam.

'Maybe we can change that.' Jake took a look up at the night sky. 'How long before dawn, you reckon?'

'Two hours, more or less.'

'Time enough then. You notice any dogs last time we were here?'

'Can't say I did but then I was occupied at the time.'

'If they've got a hound dog down there it'll start yelping once it gets wind of us.'

Sam licked a finger and held it up, feeling the faint breeze against the wet digit. 'Wind's towards us. Might be we'll be OK.'

'Here's the deal. I'm going inside. Can you hold the front porch for me?'

'Sure thing. How do you want to play it?'

Jake climbed to his knees. 'Aw, hell. Let's go riding in like we belong. Night herders, or something like that. Keep the horses ready at the rail out front.'

They returned to their mounts and removed their spurs against any noise, hanging them over their saddle horns. Sam drew his Winchester from its scabbard and led the two of them down. They moved slowly and as silently as possible, two dark shapes gliding through the long grass on the sloping hillside. At a walk they approached the rail in front of the stone built house. All remained quiet. The interior of the shadowed porch was pitch black in the starlight.

The two dismounted, the creak of leather sounding ominously loud in the still air. Jake climbed the wooden porch steps, testing each plank before he put his full weight on it. Sam stepped up close behind, keeping the Winchester ready. Once under the porch roof, Sam slid deeper into the shadows and nodded to Jake, who silently turned the front-door handle. It was a glass panelled door, with a small lace curtain hanging over the window, hiding the interior. The door opened easily on well oiled hinges. Leeward was very sure of his position now, he had no need to fear intruders.

Jake stepped inside. He found a large carpeted lobby with arched entrances to rooms off each side. One was a lounge with heavy leather armchairs, the other a dining room, well appointed with a long polished wood table and chairs. A wide central stairway ran up to the second storey. There was the scent of fresh wax and lavender oil in the air, that and oil lamps recently extinguished. Slowly Jake climbed the stairway, the Mauser held before him.

He reached a hallway above that angled to left and right. Doors stood closed along the length of the hallway and Jake wondered which one held Kitty captive. He began to try them one by one, finding each one empty of occupants. He travelled the length of the right-hand corridor without any luck and was about to start down the other side when he heard the sound of raucous snoring. It came from the far end of the left-hand hallway. Moving on the balls of his feet Jake hurried in that direction.

He pushed open the door and found himself in a bedroom. A huge double bed was occupied and it was from there that the sound of snoring issued. Only minimal light reached through the windows and Jake was hard put to find his way. He was at the foot of the bed when he ran into something soft with the toe of his boot. There was a small female yelp and Jake realized he had

146

tripped over a woman's form lying on the floor.

'Who's that?' asked the woman sleepily and at the sound of her voice Jake recognized Kitty.

The snoring stopped instantly with a sharp intake of breath. Jake moved quickly, bounding across the room and clambering up onto the bed. 'Don't make a move,' he hissed, pressing the pistol under the occupant's chin.

By the dim light he could see that the figure he straddled was Leeward, who lay bundled in silk sheets and surrounded by deep pillows. Bizarrely, Leeward wore a long tasselled nightcap. Jake realized with a cynical smile that he even dressed well at night.

'Kitty,' whispered Jake. 'It's me.'

Kitty breathed a long sigh of relief. 'Oh, at long last. Thank God you've come.'

Leeward remained motionless, only his head showing above the sheets.

'You stay quiet,' ordered Jake. 'Kitty, what are you doing down there?'

'He keeps me here,' Kitty said with disgust. 'Tied to the foot of his bed like a dog. Says it's where I belong and better get used to it.'

Jake bored the gun barrel deep into Leeward throat and he heard the man gurgle in soft complaint. 'He harm you?'

'Not yet,' whispered Kitty. 'But he intended to.'

Holding Leeward by the neck of his nightgown, Jake moved off the bed, pulling the man with him.

'Get down there and untie her,' he ordered in a hushed voice. 'Don't try anything foolish. I'm just looking for an excuse.'

'What are you going to do?' Leeward said boldly. 'Shoot me? You'll have a horde of bunkhouse cowboys down on you if you do.'

'Well, that won't matter much to you by then, will it?' Jake answered. 'Now get those ropes off her.'

'He's taken the ranch,' Kitty said as Leeward bent to untie her.

'I know it all, Kitty,' said Jake. 'Clay Rudebaugh told us everything.'

'Clay's alright? Oh, thank goodness. I feared he was a dead man by now.'

'No, he's back in town sitting on top of Reichter with a shotgun in his hand. Reichter's going to spill it all, Leeward. You hear that? Cole Reichter, sheriff of Oakum. What in God's name where you thinking of.'

'It seemed politic at the time,' answered Leeward coolly as the ropes fell from Kitty's wrist.

Kitty climbed to her feet and Jake could see that she wore no more than a plain, grubby shift. She rubbed her wrists, then swung a mighty right hand that cracked hard against Leeward's cheek. 'That's for all you've done, Christopher.'

Leeward pulled off his nightcap and stood rubbing his cheek. 'There's no way out, you realize, the two of you? I'll have you hounded down. I'll make sure you pay for this in the worst possible ways I can think of.'

'I don't think so,' warned Jake. 'You're going back to sit alongside Reichter until it's trial time.'

'What can you hold against me? I've done nothing.'

'I can think of a few things you're a party to,' snapped Kitty. 'Assaulting poor Clay, murdering Sheriff Deeling, let alone the misuse of your position as mayor to bring in those gunmen as bailiffs and then give the property to them. Any court will see you for what you are with those charges.'

Leeward snorted confidently. 'You think you can make that stick? You're out of your minds.'

'Enough!' said Jake abruptly. 'We've got to go, Kitty. Before the bunkhouse boys wake up.'

'Oh, Jake,' said Kitty, rushing into his arms. 'Jake, Jake, I missed you so.' She kissed him hard, pressing herself to his chest. Jake was pleasantly surprised, she felt good in his arms and for a moment he forgot where he was.

Leeward saw his opportunity and took it quickly. Whilst Jake's attention was distracted by Kitty he made for the door and ran shouting down the corridor.

'Murder! Murder!' he bellowed. 'Murder in the house!'

He made it down the stairs and ran out onto the porch in bounding leaps. As he burst through the front door, Sam was quickly behind him and delivered a blow to the back of Leeward's head with the flat of the Winchester. Stunned, Leeward flew forward in a tumble down the porch steps and lay in a dusty tangle, his nightshirt wrapped around him.

Lights flickered on in the bunkhouse and semi-clad men began to tumble noisily from the building as Jake and Kitty made it downstairs to the front porch. The cowboys crowded forward, pistols held ready. Sam fired a shot skywards from the rifle and the sharp crack brought the men to a standstill. From the dark shadows of the porch Sam called out his warning.

'Nobody move 'less they want to stop one!'

The men halted uncertainly, searching to find the shooter in the dark. Jake clattered onto the steps and into the plain view of the men.

'You all know me,' he called. 'Jake Rains from the Cartright spread over yonder.' He pointed down at the figure of Leeward, who was on all fours and rubbing the back of his head. 'Leeward here took this woman by force. Now if any of you boys go along with that then stand forward now and I'll deal with you myself.'

There was a restless shuffle amongst the men as they made to move forward collectively.

'I got a bead on the first one to step up,' called Sam, still hidden in the darkness.

'We're just working hands, mister,' one of them shouted back. 'We don't hold with harming womenfolk.'

Jake mollified his tone. 'I know you are, boys. Same as me. I didn't ask for any of this but I aim to take Leeward in to answer to the law for what he done. Now you can stand aside peaceable or we can go at it with pistols; either way we're going and he's going with us.'

'Guess you're putting us out of a job if you do it,' called the spokesman.

'Guess I am if you want to keep working for a bullying brute who takes it out on a helpless woman, beats up on her help and then steals her ranch from under her. That the kind of employer you like?'

The cowboys who, in the main, were decent men with a sense of chivalry about them, felt the sting of Jake's words. They had seen the way that Leeward and his men had behaved and although removed from town life they were sensible enough of his activities to be offended by Leeward's behaviour.

'Sounds like you've got it to rights,' called the cowhand. 'What do you say, fellows? We let them go?'

There were mumbled conversations amongst the men, with occasional disgruntled calls for loyalty to the L double E from those who felt they owed Leeward something. During their debate, Leeward climbed unsteadily to his feet and spoke to the men in a shaky voice.

'Don't let them take me. It's bloody murder they plan. They take me from here and I'll be found out on the prairie with a bullet in my head. Now you men have to help me, you hear?'

The men paused. 'That your plan, Rains?' one asked.

'No, that's not it. He's going in right and proper. Now Miss Kitty here will bear out all I say. Leeward had her tied to his bedpost like a dog.'

There was a disdainful murmur from the crowd. 'That a fact? He done that?'

'It's true,' said Kitty, standing forward. 'He had his men take me and bring me here prisoner. You can all guess what his intentions were.'

The cowhands looked at her frail figure clad only in the simple dirty shift and a ripple of anger ran through them.

'It's not true,' shouted Leeward. 'She's my fiancée, promised to me in marriage. Rains has her in his sights and aimed to take her and her ranch away from me. Now I pay you men good wages; you have to stand by me in this.'

'You keep hollerin', Leeward,' growled Sam with quiet

150

disgust, 'and I'm going to finish you here and now.'

The men were torn with indecision, not knowing quite which way to turn faced with the conflicting arguments. 'Look here,' said Jake at last. 'I've a solution. You fellows detail off a few of you to go along with us. We'll take Leeward and Miss Kitty into town. We've got a man holding the sheriff's office safe. That way you can see Leeward is put into the jailhouse right and proper and Miss Kitty can get cleaned up and some decent clothes put on her. Then we leave it for the law to decide. There's a circuit judge due any day now.'

The compromise seemed to meet with general approval and two men volunteered to accompany them into town as soon as they had breakfasted. It meant a tiresome wait but whilst the men were getting their fill, Jake saw to it that Kitty was more suitably covered with a long coat from Leeward's wardrobe and he himself was allowed to shed his nightshirt and get dressed.

'This is foolishness, Rains,' Leeward wheedled, whilst Jake watched him as he dragged on a waistcoated suit. Even in distress he was not above forgetting how he should appear. 'I can see you get the ranch back. I have the power to do it. Everything can be as it was. Why make all this fuss?' His reasonable tone did not fool Jake for a moment.

'Just hitch up your pants and keep quiet,' Jake ordered. 'Count yourself lucky it's a jail cell you're getting and not a pine box.'

'You're a fool,' Leeward snarled angrily, reverting to his real self. 'Do you think it's going to be that easy? I won't be in a prison cell long enough for you to draw breath. I'll have the best lawyer in the state defending me before I'm done.'

Jake was sorely tempted to lash out at the man, partly because he realized that what he had said was probably true, but he bit his lip and controlled himself. Jake knew that money spoke volumes when it came to the law and Leeward was well provided for in that area. However he had to believe that they had enough evidence to make it impossible for even the most biased judge to

151

acquit Leeward and his cronies.

'Just get down those stairs and find yourself a horse. We're leaving now whether those cowpokes are ready or not.'

It was early mid-morning by the time they eventually got to Oakum. The two accompanying cowboys hovered on horseback outside the jailhouse, still curious to see how things panned out. Jake took Leeward by the arm and hustled him up the board-walk to the sheriff's office, whilst Sam helped Kitty down and handed the reins from her borrowed horse over to the waiting cowboys.

'Thanks boys,' he said. 'Guess we can handle it from here.'

They shrugged awkwardly and hesitated, cowboys generally being incorrigible gossips and, short of any news of note other than cards and cattle, they still wanted to see what would happen here and then carry the information back to the others at the ranch.

'Well,' said Sam, a little irritably. 'You can get along now.'

'Guess we'll go chow down over at the eating-house a spell,' one answered.

'We already waited long enough on you already whilst you ate breakfast,' growled Sam.

'Well,' the cowboys said insolently with a firmness not to be diverted. 'Then we'll have another one.'

'Suit yourselves.' Sam shrugged, realizing he was not about to get any change out of them as he followed Jake into the office.

Clay was standing awkwardly in front of the door to the cells when he entered. He held the shotgun broken open and couched in his good hand, and wore a numbed look on his face which Sam at first put down to the effects of his stroke.

'You alright, Clay?' asked Jake, obviously also noticing some-thing.

'I . . . I'm sorry, Jake,' Clay muttered.

The office door was slammed shut behind them and Buck Holdall stood behind it, his pistol raised.

'Howdy gents.' He beamed and nodded at his boss. 'Mr Leeward.'

Clay was roughly pushed aside as the door to the cells was brusquely opened and Lorn Chaser and Cole Reichter stepped in, pistols held high.

'What have we here?' said Reichter, grinning smugly. 'Looks like the boot's on the other foot now, don't it, Rains?'

'Well, well, boys,' Leeward greeted them with a broad smile. 'Am I glad to see you. How did you get to be here?'

'Aw,' said Buck. 'Just paying a social visit on old Cole here.'

'They ran out of liquor,' offered Reichter; his earlier confidence had returned now that he had the backing of two more guns. 'And the store was closed.'

Buck nudged Sam in the back with his gun barrel. 'Hardware on the table. Nice and easy if you please.' He leered momentarily at Kitty. 'Real nice to see you again, Miss Kitty.'

As they shed their weapons, Jake had to agree with him there. Standing in the morning light with nothing but a thin shift under the coat to cover her obvious curves she certainly looked a picture.

Leeward also noticed their appreciative stares and he moved over to take Kitty's arm with a brisk air of ownership. 'So, Kitty. I think we'll be heading back to the ranch now. We have some unfinished business to attend to and we can leave the boys to take care of things here, I think.'

Jake did not hesitate, he stepped forward and hit Leeward hard. A blow that snapped Leeward's head back and sent him staggering.

Buck moved quickly, pressing the barrel of his gun to Jake's head. He snapped back the hammer loudly. 'Steady now, Jake,' he whispered. 'Let's not rush things here.'

'That's right,' growled Reichter. 'I've got a score to settle with these two. And they're going to pay for it in aces.'

Leeward looked daggers at Jake as he rubbed his jaw and wiped blood from his split lip. 'Take them somewhere out of my sight and finish them,' he hissed, his face a taut picture of hate.

'Oh, Jake. . . .' sobbed Kitty.

Unexpectedly, the office door opened wide and one of the cowboys from the ranch stood there, a surprised, questioning look on his face.

'What's going on here?' he managed before a startled Buck whirled around and firing at point-blank range, shot the man in the chest.

The cowboy tumbled backwards through the open door and out into the street. Jake and Sam both took instinctive advantage of the moment. Sam shouldered Reichter sideways into Lorn Chaser as Jake slammed Buck into the door, catching his forehead a stunning blow on the open edge. Then the two of them bolted through the opening.

The other ranch hand was outside, kneeling over his fallen companion. He looked up with consternation as Jake and Sam ran past. 'Get clear!' shouted Jake in warning as he pounded away along the boardwalk. There was a roar of rage from behind them as Lorn Chaser and Reichter rushed out and loosed off wild shots after the two running figures.

Jake and Sam ducked down an alleyway alongside the hardware store as bullets hacked explosive splinters from the plank walls around them.

'We need weapons,' shouted Sam as they ran.

'Round back here,' called Jake, steering a path to the delivery doors at the rear of the store.

The storekeeper stood there bemused, a bucket of waste in his hands. 'What's going on? I heard shots. . . .'

But Jake and Sam rushed past him and into the interior without a word.

'Hey!' the storeman called after them, 'What're you doing? You can't go in there!'

Jake ran directly to the gun counter, where a display of pistols lay under glass. 'Ammo, Sam,' he shouted as he kicked the locked glass panel open and delved for a pair of pistols. Sam lunged for the shelves behind and hoisted down a handful of card cartridge boxes. Hesitating only a moment, he also lifted a shiny new Winchester down from a rack on the wall. The two of them crouched down behind the counter, Jake spilling cartridges on the floor and filling the pistol's cylinders.

'You staying with that?' he asked as Sam crammed rounds into the rifle.

'Sure am,' Sam said, cranking a shell into the chamber.

Jake stuffed bullets into his pants pocket. 'You ready?' he asked.

Sam nodded and they both wormed their way to the front of the store where large windows looked out onto the street.

'Listen, you men. This ain't right. . . .' called the clerk from behind them.

'You'd best get out of here,' snapped Jake. 'Unless you want to get your head blown off.'

The clerk hesitated a moment, took one look at the spilled cartridges on the floor and the two determined men and decided discretion was the better part of valour. He hurried out through the back door.

'You see them?' Jake asked, staring out of the dusty window.

'Chaser's on the far side. Can't see Reichter.'

'Do we stay or go outside?' Jake asked.

'Prefer being in the open.'

'OK, let's split up.'

'Right, I'll go for Chaser. You go out the back and work around.'

As Jake hurried out of the back exit Sam tried the front door to the store and found it open. He pushed the door a crack and slid the Winchester out. He levelled the rifle, bringing Chaser into his sights as the gunfighter moved cautiously along the opposite side of Main Street. Sam fired. The round sent Chaser's hat flying before bursting a hanging oil lamp behind him. Chaser turned in a gunman's crouch, fanning the hammer and loosing off a series of shots in Sam's direction. Cursing himself for missing, Sam burst through the store door and stood on the boardwalk outside, levering the Winchester into rapid fire from his waist.

The plate glass window beside Sam blew apart and fell with a crash from Chaser's heavy barrage and the whine of passing bullets hummed around Sam. He stood his ground and continued shooting until Chaser suddenly bucked and spun into the wall behind him. Slowly the gunman slid limply to the ground.

Sam began to reload, then, suddenly he found himself lying on the boardwalk staring at the cracks in the woodwork. For a moment he wondered dazedly how he'd got there and then he felt the searing pain in his head. He rolled over to see Reichter walking towards him along the boardwalk, his smoking pistol held out straight in front of him. Reichter's teeth were bared into a cross between a grin and a snarl as he cocked the pistol and fired again. Sam rolled to one side as the bullet gouged wood from where he had just been lying. Reichter came on, shouting curses as he continued to fire.

Blood from the head wound flowed into Sam's eyes, making it difficult for him to see where his rifle was. The weapon had flown from his hand when he had fallen, knocked down by the glancing shot.

As Reichter crossed over the entrance to the alleyway beside the store, marching intently towards Sam, Jake came around the opposite end.

He saw the sheriff standing in the sunlight and called out. 'Here, Reichter!'

The gunman turned and his jaw dropped as he saw Jake with two raised pistols in his hand. Jake fired from each handgun, once, twice, three times. Each slug caught Reichter high in the body and twisted him from side to side as they struck. Reichter collapsed into the street, raising a cloud of road dust that shone like gold in the morning sunlight.

Jake ran to the alley entrance, covering the body of Reichter with his pistols as he ran. He risked a glance around the corner and saw Sam, his face covered with blood, struggling to crawl over to his Winchester. In a leap, Jake was on the boardwalk and at Sam's side.

'Come on, partner,' he said, stuffing the pistols into his belt and catching Sam under the armpits. Heaving the heavy man, he dragged him back inside the shattered store. Sam rubbed at the blood on his face, trying to clear his eyes. 'My gun,' he croaked. 'Get me my gun.'

Jake pressed one of the two pistols into his hand as he looked at the gash on Sam's forehead.

'You'll live,' he diagnosed. 'Going to have one hell of a headache though.'

'Already got it,' Sam groaned. 'Feels like he took the top of my head off.'

'Well, you're in a better state than he is right now.'

'You got Reichter?'

Jake nodded. 'There's still Holdall out there and Leeward's got Kitty.'

'Come on, Rains! Come on out here.'

The call came from outside and Jake peered through the jagged edges of the broken window to see Buck Holdall standing in the middle of the deserted street. Blood ran from the crack he had received when Jake slammed him into the door and it marked his handsome face with a vivid line of red.

'You and me, Rains. Do it if you've got the guts.'

'Don't go, Jake,' warned Sam. 'He's professional. He'll cut you down soon as look at you if you try facing him man to man.'

Jake looked out at the waiting gunman. Holdall stood confidently in the sunlight, his weapon holstered and his thumbs resting easily in his gunbelt. 'Come on, boy!' he jeered. 'Big ex-soldier like you. Climbed San Juan Hill, didn't you? Let's see if you can do the real thing without an army behind you.'

Jake stood up straight and checked the load in his six shooter, emptying the dead cases and reloading fresh ones.

157

'Don't,' said Sam again. 'Take him from here.'

Jake looked down at Sam and smiled slowly.

'Never was much of a quick-draw artist.' With that he aimed through the broken window and fired directly at Holdall where he stood centre street.

The shoulder padding of Holdall's jacket sleeve flapped open as the bullet tore through and the gunman turned sideways, pulling his firearm out as he did so. A look of surprise showed on his face. 'Thought you had more moxie than that, Rains,' he shouted. He fired at the shadowed figure in the store.

Jake ducked down. 'Damn!' he hissed at Sam. 'Missed him.'

Bullets continued to burst into the store as Holdall walked steadily towards them.

'Hell!' cursed Jake. 'I'll have to go out and get him after all.'

Sam thrust his pistol into Jake's hand. 'Here, take this, I can't see anything anyway.'

Taking a deep breath, Jake knelt by the door. He steadied himself a moment before diving headlong through it. Holdall was stepping up onto the boardwalk as Jake rolled out, Holdall snapped a quick shot at the spread-eagled figure whilst Jake fired both pistols at the same time. Holdall curved over backwards and fell off the boardwalk as the rounds struck, his booted feet flew into the air and he landed solidly on the street a handsbreadth away from Reichter's still body.

As Jake climbed to his feet he could hear Holdall chuckling to himself.

'Dammit, Rains, you got me. Don't that beat all? Plugged by a lousy soldier boy.'

Jake stepped over and kicked Holdall's revolver out of reach. He looked down at the wounded man, a bleeding tear in each shattered shoulder.

'Sam,' he called. 'Get out here and watch this fellow, will you? I'm about to go get Miss Kitty.'

'He's holed up in the jailhouse,' Holdall supplied, wincing as he shuffled painfully. 'Got himself a gun too. So be careful, Jake.'

'Obliged,' said Jake. 'You just keep still there.'

'Don't worry, Jake. I ain't going nowhere. Mind you, I'd rather be a piece or two away from old Cole here. He never was much of a one for hygiene.'

'I know it,' said Jake, his concentration elsewhere as he moved off in the direction of the sheriff's office.

The street was empty but Jake noticed anxious faces watching from windows along the way. All the townsfolk were staying inside for safety's sake whilst the gunplay went on. He saw that the L double E cowpoke had moved his downed friend away from the front of the jail and the way was clear to enter. As he approached, though, the office door opened and Clay and Kitty came out, followed by Leeward, Clay's shotgun held in his hand and pointed at Jake over their shoulders.

'Step aside, Rains!' Leeward called.

'Can't do that,' Jake answered.

'We're going down to the livery. You just step out of the way or one of these two will get it.'

In answer, Jake raised a pistol and cocked back the hammer, aiming carefully at Leeward.

'Nobody's going anywhere,' Jake said calmly.

Leeward cocked both hammers on the double-barrelled. 'I mean it,' he warned nervously, and Jake could see that he did. The desperation in his face was plain to see as his finger tightened on the trigger and Jake knew he was about to fulfil his promise. Jake hesitated; he could not risk hitting Kitty or Clay, Leeward was too well covered by both their bodies.

Then Jake caught Clay's eye and watched the slight nod of his head. With an upward movement of his good hand Clay nudged the shotgun barrel upwards as Leeward fired. The boom of both barrels filled the street and the shot went high in the air. At the same moment, Clay pushed Kitty to one side and dodged away himself. Leeward's eyes opened wide in terror as he saw nothing stood between him and Jake.

Jake fired one clean shot. A round hole appeared neatly in

Leeward's forehead and instantly he collapsed in a loose heap in the road.

There was a second of silence as the sounds of gunshots died away, then Kitty was in Jake's arms, holding him tightly. Over her golden curls, Jake nodded his thanks to Clay.

'Is it over?' Kitty gasped.

'It's done,' said Jake. 'You're safe now.'

'And Sam?'

'He's alright.'

'Thank God,' She murmured looking up at him, her eyes soft and admiring. 'Jake, can we go home now?'